ALLIGATOR
BAIT
GATOR-MAN #1

Other Books by David R. Michael

Novels
Gunwitch: A Tale of the King's Coven
Gunwitch: The Witch Hunts
The Door to the Sky
The Summoning Fire

Collections
Brain Freeze & Other Stories
Demon Candy
Dragons of the Stars
The World Wears Thin

ALLIGATOR BAIT
GATOR-MAN #1

DAVID R. MICHAEL

Published By
Four Crows Landing

For Bloody Barnabas

COLD, DIRTY WATER woke Ash Turner, and filled his mouth when he tried to take to a breath and call out for Jamie—

The thought of her name was like claws dragged across his soul, but he needed to get back to her–

He choked and coughed on foul-tasting water and a more pressing need forced its way into his consciousness. He needed to not drown.

Ash closed his mouth and fought the urge to choke again as he struggled against the water that surrounded him, entangled his arms and legs, and pulled him down with its grip on his clothes. He tried to spit out the water, but more rushed in.

His eyes opened, but he saw nothing. His choke tried to become a scream.

There was no up or down for him any more, only a black, watery void. But not an empty void. The void looked back at him and demanded … something. The claws in his soul tugged at him, but offered no assistance.

A part of his brain tried to remember how he had ended up in the water while the rest of him flailed and fought against both memory and water.

Say 'hello' to the gators for–

The rest of the big man's words were lost in the noise, heat and pain of a pistol discharging into the back of Ash's head.

He didn't know the big man's name. They had never been introduced. But he remembered Big Man had not been the one who shot him. That had been Big Man's sneering partner. Both Big Man and Sneer had their guns out, but it had been Sneer, out of sight behind Ash as he knelt on the rotten wood of the old dock, who had pulled the trigger. Sneer was always interrupting Big Man.

Ash didn't remember falling forward into the dirty water off the side of the dock, but it must have happened.

Somehow, thinking that his current situation had a knowable cause calmed Ash. He regained enough control over his limbs to reach with his hands in all directions, twisting in the water, seeking one of the poles that held up the dock. If he could just find one of the poles, he could climb up and pull himself out of the water. Even if Big Man and Sneer were still there, ready to push him back in. Or shoot him again. It didn't matter. He would pull himself up. He had to.

Ash tasted warm blood in the water. One of his hands went to feel the back of his head, even as he realized, somehow, that the blood wasn't his. Wasn't even human. He tasted the blood again before he could stop himself, his lips separating to let in more of the tainted water, his tongue touching the roof of his mouth, the taste becoming an untagged memory in his mind, waiting to be identified.

Now Ash fought the urge to vomit.

Light stabbed into the water from above him, distracting him from the nausea and creating an "up" for him to strive toward. The light was not directly above him, and not moving like a flashlight would, so he did not think it was Big Man and Sneer looking for him. But even if the two men were the source of the light, Ash decided he wanted to breathe at least once more.

His right hand first, then his head, came out of the water and he exhaled the breath he had been holding and took in a damp new breath that made him choke. He flailed on the surface, treading water, squinting against the glare as he tried to get his bearings. He heard the laughter of two men, and he almost dove back under the water. The voices were different, though. Not Big Man and Sneer. Ash choked again as he laughed in relief. He tasted his own salty tears in the fetid water around him.

The light was two yellow headlights striking at him from at least twenty feet away. An old Ford pickup was parked on a slight rise, its headlights pointing down at the edge of the pool and the thrashing body of a white-tail buck.

Ash raised his left hand to wave, to attract the attention of whoever was in the truck, but at the sight of the deer, the blood-taste-memory returned to the forefront of Ash's mind, and became stronger as the buck continued to bleed out into the water. Bile rose in Ash's throat at the thought of tasting the buck's blood. And the thought of clamping his teeth down on its flesh–

"–ing see that?" asked one of the men in the truck. The windows were rolled down. Ash smelled cigarette smoke.

"Yeah, I fucking saw that," said the other man. "Heard it too, you redneck bastard."

"Boom!"

"Yeah, 'boom'."

"Boom, boom, boom! Right in the heart!"

"Yeah. Next time hang out the fucking window so I don't go fucking deaf, yeah?"

"Yeah, yeah. Pussy."

The doors of the pickup opened and two men dressed in hunter gear stepped out. The man from the passenger side wore booted waders up to his chest and carried a rifle in both hands. The driver also carried a rifle, but he held it down, the barrel along his right leg.

"Hey!" Ash shouted. "Help me!" He pushed thoughts of raw, bloody venison from his mind and kicked toward the shore. He moved through the water faster than he expected, then tripped as his foot caught on a root in the shallows. He splashed and stumbled his way to the shore beside the dying buck. "Help," he said again, on his hands and knees, spitting out dirty, buck-blood-tasting water. "Help me. I've been … shot."

"Yeah?" said the driver. "Well I guess we know where one of those two extra 'booms' went now, don't we? Yeah, we do."

"Shut up, Decker."

Ash pushed himself up so he was on his knees. He smiled, panting, just happy to be alive. Then his smile faltered.

The two men stood far enough apart that he couldn't look at them both at the same time. They regarded him with serious expressions. The driver shifted his rifle so he held it with both hands, the barrel almost–but not quite–pointed at Ash.

"You shut up, Dewalt," the driver said. "But he ain't shot. That's just mud and buck blood."

Ash looked down at himself. He still wore his light blue Oxford shirt, but it wasn't blue anymore, and there were multiple rips across his chest. At least half the buttons up the front had been torn free. The cuffs at his wrists, though, were still held together by the little, white buttons, as if he had just done them up. The dirty water and the blood of the deer had stained the shirt, and the torn remnants of the once-white undershirt he wore beneath it. His casual trousers were in the same state as the undershirt, torn in multiple places, and streaked with mud and blood. His hand went to the back of his head. He felt only wet hair. Not a gaping bullet wound. Not even a scratch. He pulled his hand back to look at his fingers. Nothing but mud.

How had he survived a shot to the back of his head?

"You ain't shot, you dumb townie tourist," Decker said. "At least, not yet."

"Yeah. Not shot yet, are you?"

Ash realized he must have spoken, but he ignored the men. He felt the back of his head with both hands. Still no wound. But Big Man and Sneer, working for Jamie's father–

This time, along with the claws tearing at his soul and squeezing him around the neck, the thought of Jamie brought back memories of the woman. He could almost see her in front of him, the first time he had seen her, black hair flowing around her face in the cool February breezes that accompanied the Krewe of Cleopatra parade along St. Charles. Jamie was more of an empress than any of the costumed, made up women on the floats or walking alongside. Bead necklaces rained down around Jamie like glittering flowers in the rain. Her eyes had met his, and she had smiled and waved at him and called him Marcus. Then she had disappeared into the crowd, pulling on the arm of the man she was with. Ash had stood there with her flashing smile still dazzling his eyes, the warmth of her unexpected hug, and the kiss on his cheek, chasing away the chill of the damp evening and making him wish his name really was Marcus. Now, as then, he knew he had to find her. Again.

He had to get back to Jamie. He needed Jamie. Or Jamie needed him. The claws in his mind turned his thoughts of Jamie into a jumble, a puzzle put together incorrectly. Pieces of himself jammed together with ill-fitting seams.

"What happened to you, townie?" Decker asked, looking past Ash, then around at the moss-covered cypress and oaks. "You fall off a swamp tour or something?"

"Heh, yeah." Dewalt chuckled. "You fall off a swamp tour? One of those pretty little pontoon boats with all the plastic seats, yeah? And the baby gator?"

Ash stared at the men, barely understanding their words. Thoughts of Jamie–and the need to get back to Jamie–were too loud in his mind. The claws seemed to be dragging at him now, pulling at him, trying to yank him into motion.

"Did you get to hold the baby gator, townie?" As he talked, Decker stepped to his right, further away from Dewalt. He shifted his grip on his rifle. Now the barrel pointed at ground in front of Ash. "Or did you get so scared you fell of the boat?"

"Yeah, is that what happened?" Dewalt mirrored Decker's movement, stepping to his left. He still held his rifle more casually, not actually pointing at anything, but his voice took on a harder tone. "It is, yeah, isn't it? Did you wet your pants, townie? Did that baby gator scare you so bad, yeah? Then you jumped off the boat to cover for it?"

"Jamie," Ash said. "I need … to get back …"

"Well now, Jamie," Decker said, "I think you already missed your ride."

"Yeah," Dewalt said. "I think you done already missed your ride." In a smooth, practiced motion, Dewalt brought up his rifle and aimed along the sights at Ash.

Ash put his hands out. "Wait–"

"Hold on, Dewalt." Decker moved his rifle so the barrel rested on his right shoulder, then settled back on his heels. He pointed with his left hand at Dewalt. "Hold your fucking fire."

"I thought–"

"Stop thinking, alright? You suck at it."

"Yeah? I suck at it?" Dewalt glared at Decker, but his rifle was rock steady, still pointed at Ash. "Who kept pulling the damn trigger inside the fucking cab of the truck? Boom boom boom? That was you, wasn't it? Yeah, it was."

Decker made a dismissive gesture. "Shut up. If this townie did fall off a tour boat, then there's gonna be a search party. If he's shot, they're gonna know it wasn't just gators got him."

"Only if they find him."

Decker didn't say anything, just looked at Ash, as if considering possible options.

"Yeah, yeah," Dewalt said after a few seconds. "Fine. I'll cover him for you."

Ash staggered to his feet, hands still palm out in front of him. The muddy ground in front of him rose at an angle from the bank of the pool, making it difficult to stand. He faced Decker, so he wouldn't be staring into Dewalt's rifle muzzle. "Look, I just need a ride back to New Orleans."

"You just stop right there, townie," Dewalt shouted at his back. "Yeah, you just fucking stand still."

Ash kept his gaze on Decker. "I didn't see anything—"

"Yeah?" Dewalt said. "What didn't you see?"

Before he could stop himself, Ash turned to look at the dead buck.

"Yeah, that's what I thought you didn't see."

As he turned to face Decker again, Ash looked past the pickup, avoiding the glare of the headlights. A narrow mudslide snaked down the incline. Ash followed it up with his eyes and saw a break in the undergrowth at the crest of the small ridge, like a game trail.

"I just need to get back to Jamie," Ash said, looking Decker in the eye. The man's expression showed only a touch of curiousity. More impatience, as if he were just waiting for

Ash to stop talking. "She … I … need …" The words jumbled in his head.

"Too bad for little Jamie, I guess," Decker said. "You know what, Dewalt? I think we should just kill him and leave him for the gators. I've already spotted one or two just waiting for him. Or for us to clear out and leave them that juicy buck."

The skin along Ash's chin tingled, then a chill went down his spine. They were going to shoot him. Just like Big Man and Sneer had already done once tonight.

"Sounds good to me, brother–"

The sound started as a low growl in Ash's chest, but quickly amplified into a scream. He might have screamed Jamie's name, but he wasn't sure. He just threw the sound of his anger, fear and frustration straight at Decker, then launched himself sideways, to his right.

He felt the passage of the bullet and heard the sound of the gunshot simultaneously. He felt a burning pain crawl in slow motion across his left arm, as Decker stepped back, also in slow motion. The pain spurred Ash. His feet found perfect purchase on the muddy bank and the muscles of his legs propelled him past the front of the pickup and in a straight line up the incline toward the game trail.

Decker and Dewalt were shouting as he crested the hill. There might have been a second gunshot, but Ash couldn't be sure over the sound of his heart pounding and his heavy breathing. Underbrush seemed to part in front of him as he ran, letting him barrel through at full speed. He was sure he had never run so fast in his life.

He didn't know how long he ran, only that he ran. And then, suddenly, he wasn't running anymore. Not that he had planned to stop. Instead, his body just … gave out. His legs buckled and he stumbled and fell on his belly and slid on mud until he came to a stop on the muddy bank of another pool.

Between deep, panting, burning breaths, he managed to push himself over and onto his back. He stared at the leafy, mossy foliage overhead and tried to listen for the sounds of pursuit. He saw no sign of the headlights from the pickup truck, nor did he hear the roar of its engine or the sound of pursuit on foot. The bayou was far from silent around him, but his were the only man-made sounds that touched his eardrums.

He couldn't see anything but trees and bushes and water, but he could feel the eyes of the bayou looking at him. Living eyes, watching eyes, appraising eyes, keeping their distance, but watching him.

After a few minutes, finally catching his breath, he pushed himself to his feet. His legs still shook from his recent exertion, but they held him up. He had no idea which direction he should head, so he chose to go right, to walk perpendicular to the route he had run. He stumbled along the edge of the water, into the swampy darkness.

He felt the eyes he couldn't see watching him as he walked.

2

ASH WALKED BESIDE the gray stretch of highway, head down against the rain, face turned away from the wind. He was walking blindly forward, but heading south according to the periodic signs that proclaimed US 51 South.

It was as dark along the highway as it had been in the swamp. He had no idea what time it was or even how long he had been walking. He could hear the sounds of heavy traffic racing above him on I-55, held up out of his reach by tall viaducts. He kept hoping he would find an on-ramp or off-ramp or any other kind of ramp that would let him climb up to the interstate. Maybe on the interstate he would no longer feel the swamp watching him.

There was almost no traffic where he was walking. Only three vehicles had passed him since he had emerged from the swamp, and two of those had been heading the wrong way. Away from New Orleans. Away from Jamie.

"I have to get to Jamie," he told the red lights of the sedan that whipped past him and disappeared around the next eastward bend of the highway.

The rain had soaked him, as if he had been dunked in the bayou again, but at least it had washed off most of the mud from the swamp. The rain had also washed away the blood from where the bullet grazed his left arm, and that of the buck, as well. He had not found any wound on him from being shot by Sneer. But if there had been such a wound, and that wound had bled, Ash was sure the rain would have washed it away, as well. He was as clean as the rain could make him.

He wondered that he didn't shudder. The cold rain plus the wind should make him shudder. He wondered if he was going into hypothermic shock. The cold made him want to sleep, which he resisted by plodding forward, but didn't seem to touch him, otherwise.

He remembered shuddering at the cold before, when Big Man and Sneer had pulled him from their black SUV and pushed him along the dock to where they had made him kneel, before they shot him. He had shuddered before that, too, when the two men had found him with Jamie, naked.

Big Man and Sneer had burst in while Ash and Jamie were making love. They had pulled him off her, and held them both at gunpoint as Ash put on his clothes. Ash remembered babbling something about them both being adults, and her father couldn't run her whole life. No one had paid him any attention. Big Man and Sneer were shouting at him to get the fuck dressed, and Jamie had been screaming at the men that they didn't have to do this, that Ash wasn't the one. She had threatened to call her father, then started to do so, but Big Man had taken her phone from her.

Yes, Mr. Derouen, Big Man had said when the man at the other end answered. Jamie was screaming to let her talk to her father, but Big Man paid her no attention. *We have him. Yes, sir, Mr. Der–*

Shut up! Sneer had shouted at Jamie, waving his gun in her face, interrupting Big Man.

You couldn't wait two more seconds before shouting at her? Big Man had asked after he ended the call with Jamie's father. *Two fucking seconds?*

She was bugging me. And she was yelling while you were on the phone with the boss.

You were yelling louder than she was–

Come on, asshole, Sneer had shouted at Ash, waving the gun again, but with visibly more intent to actually pull the trigger than before. *You have a date. Another date.* He had laughed, a sound as cold as the water that now washed over Ash. *A date with the divine.*

That had set off Jamie again, but neither Big Man nor Sneer paid her any attention. *I'm sorry,* she had said to Ash as he was pulled out of her apartment. Sneer had held her back. *I'm sorry. I told you to call after Mardi Gras.* Then Sneer had pulled the door of her apartment shut and Ash had not seen her again.

"You OK, man?" The shouted words pulled Ash back to the present. A small car had come alongside him and was crawling forward at Ash's slow, cold pace. The window of the passenger side window was down. The driver was a thin man, tall enough that he had lean over to look through the window at Ash. His gray eyes looked into Ash's. "You don't look high or stoned." Before Ash could respond, the man went on. "You wreck your car or something? You need a ride?"

Ash stopped walking and the car's break lights cast a bright red light behind them as the car came to a stop as well. "Jamie," he said, finding it hard to form his need into a sentence. "I need ... I need to get ... to Jamie."

"Jamie, eh?" The driver's eyes showed some amusement, though the rest of his face was all concerned attentiveness. "Do you know where Jamie lives?"

Ash nodded. He knew the exact address, but all that came out of his mouth was, "New Orleans."

The driver's lips curled into a tight smile. "Oh, good. So you're almost there." His left hand pushed a button and Ash heard the passenger door unlock. "Get on in, man. We'll see if Jamie's home."

Ash opened the door. A few rumpled takeout bags littered the floor of the car, but the seat was clear. Ash started to step in, then realized he was dripping wet, and paused.

The driver waved at him to climb in. "Get in, man. You aren't getting any drier, and I can assure you that seat has seen much worse than you. I don't always pick up strays," he added, "but when I do, they're almost always wet and miserable. Get in."

Ash got in.

The interior smelled of stale fast food, sun-soaked plastic from the dashboard and the nearly overwhelming chemical smells of a man who had recently showered with scented shampoo and soap, but the car was warm and helped remove some of the lethargic fuzziness from Ash's mind. Still, it was hard to think beyond his need to find Jamie.

"You hungry, man? You look like a man who could use a bite to eat."

Ash's thoughts flashed back to the buck bleeding into the water. Nausea and hunger collided in his gut and he grimaced. Then he managed a nod.

"I'll take that as a yes."

Ash looked out the window as the car went past a number of service stations and closed restaurants, then up and around on an on-ramp and merged into traffic on I-10. How far had he walked? When Big Man and Sneer had driven him out of New Orleans, the trip had seemed so long. He tried to remember how close the swamps were to New Orleans. Like Decker and Dewalt had said, Ash was a tourist. He had flown into New Orleans and had no mental map of the area, except for the French Quarter, the Garden District, and the route of the St. Charles trolley. And some stores and restaurants on Canal Street.

"So what happened to you, man? You crash your car? Do you need to call anyone?" The driver picked up a phone from a tray beneath the center dash and held it out to Ash.

"Jamie," Ash said, nodding. He took the offered phone, but only held it in front of him, staring at the bright digital display. The clock said, "4:23 AM". Below the time, it displayed "Friday, February 21".

"Your phone's date," Ash started. Ten days? Big Man and Sneer had found him with Jamie on the night of the eleventh. The night before Mardi Gras. "That can't … be right."

The driver leaned over to look at the phone's display. "No, that's right. Thursday night. Well, I guess it's Friday now." He settled back into his seat.

Ash didn't respond. He just stared at the display, trying to account for lost time. Lost days. He watched the clock change to "4:24 AM". Then, "4:25 AM". The date remained "Friday, February 21."

The driver glanced at Ash again. "Are you sure you're OK, man? You look like you're in shock. Can you tell me your name?"

Without thinking, Ash responded. "Ash." Then, "Ash Turner."

"OK, Ash Turner. Why don't you tell me what happened? How did you end up on the side of the road on this dark and stormy night?"

The scene in Jamie's apartment, being dragged away from Jamie, being shot, all of it flashed in Ash's mind like the lightning that crawled through the clouds overhead. The clawing at his soul resumed and he put his hand on his chest, then on the back of his head. His words got jumbled again as he rubbed the short hairs where there was no wound. "Shot," he said. Suddenly he felt very weak. The phone fell out of his left hand.

"You were shot?"

Ash managed to nod. Hunger and fatigue and the close smells of the driver and his car threatened to suffocate him. "Shot ... swamp ... Jamie. I have to ..." He turned to look at the driver. The man met his eyes. "Ten days?"

"Calm down, man." The driver paused, then said it again, "Calm down, Ash." He reached out with his right hand and put it on Ash's shoulder. "Mr. Turner," he said, "I think Jamie's going to have to wait. You and me, we're going to the hospital."

3

ASH WALKED ALONG the south bank of a river of women's faces, half the faces looking away from him, the other half ignoring him. Between the two banks of the river a golden current moved. Women dressed in shiny, elaborate costumes, flashy imitations and painstakingly created reproductions of Egyption clothes and headdresses. Black wigs and golden snakes. Eyes of Ra stared and heads of Anubis bobbed with the stream, as if the doors of King Tut's Tomb had opened and flooded St. Charles Avenue with untold wealth and a horde of smiling women.

There were men in the crowd, of course, and policemen on horseback keeping the banks from overflowing, but Ash hardly saw them. Instead, his eyes went from one woman's face to the next, skipping the unimportant spaces between. Looking for Jamie's face.

He walked in a trance of déjà vu. It had been during the Krewes of Cleopatra parade that he had first seen Jamie. Which should have been two weeks ago, but was, somehow, tonight. Again.

Everything around him was familiar, but everything was also … wrong. He felt as if he had been yanked out of time and reinserted sideways. He had more than just 10 lost days to account for.

That this was next year's Krewes of Cleopatra parade–
"next year" to the one he had attended–he could no longer doubt. He had told Jamie that he would be there—here?—with her at next year's parade, taking the place of the asshole she had had the misfortune to go with this—last?—year. She had laughed at his use of the word "asshole" and told him Frank wasn't that bad. Then, when he reminded her that she had called Frank an asshole first, she had poked him on the nose with one finger. *You're so cute when you're jealous.*

That had been last year–

A lost year.

A year and ten days gone in a night. The vast gulf of that year yawned between the precipice of his memories and the edge of the present that he skirted now.

Ash had waited until the driver of the small car that had found him on the side of the road and rescued him from the swamp–he was sure the man had given a name, but Ash could not recall it. He had waited until the mad left before he walked out of the emergency room and into the early morning of New Orleans. The man had bought Ash some drive-thru fast food before they got to the hospital. Ash was sure he must have eaten it, but he couldn't remember that either. The same for the tweny dollar bill he had found in his pants pocket.

His time in the small car with the tall man seemed longer ago than his last night with Jamie.

He had wandered the city as it woke up with a slight Thursday night hangover. Watched as the city cleaned up and got ready for the real party that would be happening a few hours later. The day had been unusually sunny, the warmth drying Ash's torn clothes as he walked down side streets and along busy boulevards. He had not attracted any significant attention as he walked, even with his torn clothes, and he paid no attention to anyone once he realized they were not Jamie. It had taken him most of the morning to orient himself and realize he knew where he was, and, more importantly, knew how to get to Jamie's apartment from there.

She wasn't there. Her name wasn't even on the list for the building. There was only slightest hint of her smell still lingering in the air. Weeks old, at least. The doorman had been more interested in stopping Ash from sniffing the air and getting Ash to leave than providing any useful information, but he had been clear on one point: Jamie Derouen no longer lived there.

Then Ash had seen flyers for the Krewes of Cleopatra parade, just like he had … before. That had been the beginning of the déjà vu. As if he had been given a chance to do it all over again. But this time to find Jamie on purpose, not just by happy accident.

He had come to New Orleans alone last year. Recently divorced from– He could almost picture the woman's face in the shattered mirror of his memories. And even more recently he had been laid off from– He had been … an accountant, maybe? Or a computer programmer? Whoever, whatever, he had been before, suddenly he had been possessed of more time than ever in his life to do nothing with. It had then been the middle of January, so the opportunity to seek a new beginning in the new year had been taken away from him along with his job. Then he had heard of Mardi Gras, how it was happening early. He had always throught of Mardi Gras as just a day on the calendar that other people celebrated. Then he discovered that it was more than just one day. It was practically a season, if you went to the right places. And easily the most right place of all for Mardi Gras was New Orleans.

His first night in the city had been a Friday then, as well. The night of the Krewes of Cleopatra parade. A night when hundreds of women went on parade.

But he had seen only one.

Jamie had been standing on the opposite side of the street from him, her black hair adrift around her face in the evening breeze. Once he had seen her he no longer saw any of the floats nor the hundreds of other brightly-dressed women. Nor anyone else. Not even the man whose arm she held. There was something in the way she held the man's arm, how she stood beside him but separate from him, that told Ash everything he needed to know. The man could be ignored. Even when the man leaned down and said something that made her laugh, Ash knew she laughed for him, for Ash.

She did not see Ash, though, until the parade was over, and he pushed his way across the street, and, somehow, ended up standing in front of her. Him stumbling out of the crowd, her standing there like she had been waiting for him.

Hi, he had been about to say, breathless.

Marcus! she had shouted in joy, preempting him. She had shaken herself free of the invisible man beside her and thrown her arms around Ash. The hug, the feel of her body against his, almost knocked him over. But she held his shoulders and kept him upright. *It is so good to see you!*

Ash had opened his mouth to say … he had no idea what he might have said. Before he could say anything, she interrupted him again, *I have to run, but you look me up after Mardi Gras, OK?*

We don't have time for this, Jamie, the invisible man had said, or something similar. His words were as easy to ignore as the rest of him. Except her name. Ash heard her name. We need to go.

With her hands still on Ash's shoulders, she had only

glanced over her shoulder at the man, then said, *Don't be an asshole, Frank.* Then she looked at Ash again. She leaned forward and kissed Ash on the cheek. *It is so good to see you again, Marcus. Don't forget to look for me. After Mardi Gras. Bye!*

And then she had been gone, leaving behind only her scent, the touch of her lips on his cheek, and her first name.

You can't go stalking a girl based on her first name, someone had said to Ash. A friend? His best friend? On the phone.

Still in a daze, Ash had called his best friend– Phillip? Yes. Phillip Oliver, the man Ash had known since college, the best man at Ash's wedding—and the first to hear about the divorce–whose face suddenly seemed out of reach in the broken memories that predated Jamie. You can't just go to Google and type in 'Jamie'. How many–

Eighty-seven million, Ash had said. But they don't all live in New Orleans.

Ash crossed Jackson Avenue behind the barricades and the press of spectators. He was very near where he had lived that one incredible moment, where he had met Jamie, when a stray gust of wind hit him in the face. He stopped. Through the scents of a thousand people and several dozen horses, through the smells of grease and urine and horse manure, he smelled Jamie. For an instant. For one shallow breath. Then it was gone.

No longer adrift, Ash pushed his way through the people massed behind the barricade. He ignored the elbows and shoulders that tried to stop him until his waist was pressed against the cold metal of the fence-like barricade. He scanned the far side of the street with his eyes as he continued to take in deep breaths through his nose–

A horse stepped in front of Ash. "You need to step back, sir," said the uniformed policeman mounted on the horse. The horse looked at Ash, blew out of its nose, then tried to pull away. The policeman held it in place.

Ash pushed to his right, forcing a woman back, elliciting another loud protest he ignored. He looked around the horse's neck, looking for one bright face.

"Don't make me get down off my horse, sir."

"Jamie!" Ash shouted when he saw her across the wide street.

Ash threw his leg over the barrier, startling the horse so it pulled back. Then Ash was past the barricade, ducking under the horse's nose, and running across the intersection.

The horse whinnied and the policeman shouted, "God damn it, man! Get back here!"

Ash ran in front of a float that looked like a double-decker cloud bus with a jazz band playing on the first level and people throwing beads and coins from the top. The sharp sound of a police whistle pierced the sounds of the crowd and the music.

Another mounted policeman, this one guarding the far side of the parade path, tried to move in front of Ash, but his horse shied and pulled away as Ash got near. The people at the barricade, though, didn't move. Ash forced his way over the barricade, pushing people out of his way. His left foot caught on the top of the barricade and he fell. A hard fist struck him on the right side of his head on the way down. Scrambling in an underbrush of ankles and trousers, more than one booted foot kicked him. More than one sharp heel stabbed at his hands. But he was able to get to his feet and push his way through.

He burst out of the jungle of angry people into a small, clear space. Jamie stood there, as if she had been waiting for him.

"Jamie!" he shouted again.

Her black hair was different now, shorter, waved with curls and streaked with red. Her face, though, was exactly the same. Smooth and perfect and–

"Ash?" she said as her pale skin went the color of his name. Her brown eyes went wide and she stumbled back into the arms of the invisible, ignorable man.

"You again?" Frank said, pushing Jamie behind him.

Ignoring Frank, Ash stepped forward, reached out with his right hand. A long scratch across his knuckles leaked blood.

"Jamie! I–"

The ignorable man's right fist hit Ash in the mouth, the unexpected impact jerking Ash's head to the right and spinning him in place. He stumbled and fell against the backs of the people he had just fought free of.

He seemed incapable of freeing himself this time. Arms and legs entangled him and held him. Another fist struck him in the back just as another police whistle burst through the white noise of the shouts and screams and music of the parade.

Ash tried to breathe, tried to call out for Jamie again, to make sure she understood how much he needed her, but it was as if all the oxygen were out of his reach. He gasped, his mouth opening and closing like a fish out of water. His vision tunnelled as if he were falling down a long, long sewer pipe. Someone grabbed his arms and pulled him and he found he no strength to resist.

Suddenly he could see the black water of the bayou at night rushing at his face just as it had after Sneer shot him in the back of the head. Then he saw nothing.

4

HOOKED TEETH PENETRATED the numbing nothing that should have been Ash's death. Before he could fully acknowledge this new pain, Ash felt himself torn free of the blackness with a jerk that tried to break him in half. Then he was thrashing about in the dark, lifeless waters of nowhere, fruitlessly fighting the grip of the invisible jaws and teeth.

Sharp claws joined the teeth and pulled at the flimsy remnants of his substance and ripped it apart. Ash would have screamed, but he was dead. He couldn't scream. He could only feel the agony, not release it or express it.

Then, as suddenly as they had grabbed him, the teeth and claws released him and he floated, lost in himself and from himself. He drifted in this new blackness, unsure who he even meant when he thought of "himself". He could see his memories, see who he was, but only as shredded tapestries. The substance of both became thinner as he floated, lost in this dark eternity that his agnostic upbringing had left him completely unprepared for. His awareness became like that of an insomniac, unable to find comfort, hoping for oblivion.

He had no idea how much time had passed when the teeth returned, and the claws. His new struggles were as fruitless as those before. He could only wish he could scream as he felt himself being pulled apart, felt teeth tearing and grinding, felt himself examined and tasted. Swallowed and consumed. He became less and less, but the pain he could not express remained a constant, the only part of the blackness he could feel.

Then, like a curtain being torn away, the blackness was gone and what was left of Ash Turner was vomited forth into the light.

After a dizzying eternity, he could see a body sprawled forward, face down, suspended, floating. An invisible current pushing against the body, tilting it, turning it so Ash could see the face.

There was no face. Only a hole where a face had once been. The lower jaw hung from a loose flap of flesh. Both eyes were open, but only one eye still existed. The other had burst and its viscera floated like the tendrils of a sea anemone.

As Ash watched, disembodied, a school of small fish swam out of the darkness. Several of the fish darted into the cavity of the face and nibbled on the torn edges. One fish's mouth closed on a tendril of the broken eye and tugged on it.

The teeth and claws found Ash again, and they pulled at him, forced him into motion, then pushed him toward the body.

Into the body.

In a rush of disjointed, broken memories and feelings and thoughts, Ash was pushed into the body–back into his own body–with a mission–a mission to find–

"Jamie!"

Ash woke, choking on his scream, sitting up so fast that his head swam. The smells of unwashed men, stale alcohol, urine, and shit hit him in the face and brought on nausea. He fell to his right, rolling on a cold concrete floor until his right cheek was pressed against the hard surface. His abdomen heaved and he tasted bile in his mouth, surprised that it wasn't dirty bayou water. He managed to avoid vomiting even as his stomach heaved again, curling him into a fetal position.

"Turner!" shouted a man's voice.

"Tina Turner?" asked another man's voice.

"Lana Turner?" asked a third.

"Ted Turner?"

"I was going to say Ike—"

"Shut up," the first voice said. "Ashley Turner. Where are you? Detective wants to speak to you."

5

Ash's fingers wrapped around the Styrofoam cup of coffee the police detective placed in front of him. The warmth that leaked through the thin insulation of the cup helped him wake up as much as breathing in the earthy scent of the steam. He had been alone in the interview room, sitting in the seat the uniformed officer told him to sit in, not moving, hardly thinking.

I need to find her, he had told the officer. The officer had only grunted in response. After the officer left him alone, Ash said nothing else. He waited. He didn't know how long. Then the detective arrived with a stack of manila folders and a single cup of coffee.

"Ashley Turner," the detective said, sitting down across from Ash. He placed the stack of folders on the table in front of him, then patted the stack, as if to make sure Ash noticed them. "The one who came back."

Ash ignored the folders and looked at the detective. "I need to find Jamie Derouen."

The man's expression didn't change. "What you need to do, Mr. Turner, is talk to me."

Ash let his gaze fall back to the cup of coffee. He picked

it up with both hands, but he could tell it was too hot to drink, even to sip, so he just held it in front of his lips and inhaled the warm steam. He could feel the warmth spreading slowly through his body, unkinking muscles sore after sleeping on the concrete floor of the drunk tank, rebooting his mind so he could think about more than his clawing need to find Jamie.

"Mr. Turner," the detective said. "Ash. May I call you Ash?" When Ash didn't respond, he added, "Look at me, Ash."

Ash looked at the man again, but continued to hold the coffee in front of his face. He tried to remember the name the man had given him along with the cup of coffee. His mind had still been moving very slowly then and the coffee had seemed far more important than trivial names. His eyes went to the man's chest, but the detective wasn't wearing a uniform. Just a regular shirt and tie, with no name tag. Ash gave up and just looked in the man's eyes.

The detective reminded Ash of his father. At least, what he could remember of his father. The stern, knowing, slightly disappointed look in the green-gray eyes. The thick, graying mustache that needed trimming as much as the heavy, graying eyebrows. Ash felt his own eyebrows furrow as he tried to remember more about his father, but the broken mirror of his memories refused to cooperate. Not even to offer additional isolated reflections.

"From what I hear, Ash," the detective said, "you already found Ms. Derouen. I hear she wasn't exactly thrilled to see you again."

The steam rising in front of Ash's face coalesced into the image of Jamie as he had seen her last night. Pale, shocked, and maybe more than a bit frightened. She had obviously not expected to see him again. Ash understood the feeling. When Big Man and Sneer had driven him out of town and into the swamps, he had never expected to see her again, either.

"In fact," the detective went on, "I don't think she *expected* to see you again. And why should she, Ash? None of the others have ever come back. You're the first."

Ash focused on the detective again.

The mustached moved as the detective's mouth became a tight smile. "That got your attention, didn't it, Ash?" He leaned forward and spoke slowly, "Before you showed up at that parade, none of the others have ever come back. Not a week later. Not a month later. Not a year later. Hell, Ash, not one in the last fifteen years."

"What are you talking about? What does this have to do with Jamie?"

The detective's eyes almost twinkled. "I'm talking about a mystery, Ash," he said. "A mystery that goes back fifteen years. At least, that's as far as I've found. Who knows?" He gave an elaborate shrug. "From what I've heard, Ms. Jamie Derouen's career as a ball-busting man-eater extends all the way back to kindergarten. A pretty little rich girl with an appetite for the hearts of men."

Ash sat up straighter. He put the coffee down carefully, then placed his hands flat on the table in front of him. "No, she's not like that—"

"Ha!" the detective shouted, interrupting him. "You arrogant little tourist. What do you know? You knew our local *femme fatale* celebrity for all of what? Two whole weeks? Before you disappeared?"

"Eighteen days—"

The detective dismissed the difference between two weeks and eighteen days with a wave of his hand. "You're not from around here, Ash. You're a *tourist*. Or you were, a year ago. New Orleans sees ten million people just like you every year. And, in some cases, also just like you, this city eats them up. You're special, though, Ash." The detective leaned forward and spoke very slowly. "You got spit back."

Ash opened his mouth to reply, then closed it again as he remembered the gap in his memory. He had been gone a year. He picked up the coffee again. This time he took a sip. Where had that year gone?

"Don't go getting a big head, though, Ash," the detective continued. "You're not *that* special. Certainly not from dating Ms. Jamie Derouen. From what I have been able to dig up, Ms. Derouen has had a new boyfriend every year for Mardi Gras. Though maybe they're more like *boy toys* now that she's crossed thirty. Do you feel like a boy toy, Ash?"

"I'm thirty-two," Ash said, surprising himself with the knowledge. He put the coffee down and stared at the light reflected on the dark surface of the liquid. He couldn't remember his birthday, but, somehow, he knew he was thirty-two years old. Or had been. A year ago. Was he thirty-three now?

The detective shrugged. "Every year a new boy toy," he said again. "And then, good Catholic girl she is, she gives up the lucky lad for Lent. And he's never seen again."

The detective sat up in his chair, then hunched over the table again. He spread the stack of folders in front of him as if he were fanning a deck of cards. "Gary Martin," he said, tapping one folder. "From Sugar Land, Texas, seen with Ms. Jamie Derouen at various Mardi Gras parades and parties in 1999. Missing." He tapped another folder. "Lawrence Davis. His friends in Piscataway, New Jersey, called him 'Larry'. Missing since 2004." His finger found another folder. "Howard Rinaldi. Howard here came all the way from Los Angeles, California, in 2005, supporting our fair city in her first Mardi Gras after Hurricane Katrina. Also missing."

He paused to look at Ash, then he picked through the folders until he found one that looked newer than the others.

"And here's your folder, Ash. Ashley Turner of Bixby, Oklahoma." He opened the folder and picked up a photo. He looked at the picture for a second, then held it up so he could see both the picture and Ash side by side. "You look a little worse for wear, Ash, but hardly a day older. And whose the little lady with you?" He finally turned the photograph around so Ash could see it.

Ash stared at the picture. He recognized it as the last portrait he and ... His mind blanked on the name of the ex-wife he knew he had. He recognized her face, though, felt the conflicted emotions of their shared history, but no name came to him. The picture had been taken a year before their divorce. Why could he remember that, and not his wife's—his *ex*-wife's—name?

He realized the detective was waiting for him to answer. "My ex-wife."

The detective turned the picture back around to give it another appraisal. "Too bad, Ash. She's a pretty one. What happened?"

Ash's mind offered up a jagged-edged collage of angry words, tears, and vague disappointments. Ash shook his head. "I don't know."

Ash thought he saw the first hint of sympathy in the detective's expression, but it was gone instantly. "Men never do, in my experience," the detective said. "It was your mother, by the way."

Ash stared at the man. "My mother?"

The detective nodded. "Your mother. She was the one who reported you missing. She actually flew out here to file in person."

Ash tried to think of his mother. Where his mother should have been was ... nothing. Not even a single shard.

"She said you were a good boy," the detective went

on, looking at the typed report before him. "But tends to let women get the better of him. Especially pretty women. But, well, don't we all?"

"Why am I here, detective?"

"You were picked up on a drunk and disorderly, Ash. Don't you remember?"

"I wasn't drunk."

"We didn't check. On the other hand, you were more than disorderly enough to make up for any blood alcohol shortfall, don't you think?" The detective did another of his elaborate shrugs. "So you got picked up and dragged in and dumped in the drunk tank, along with many others, I'm sure you noticed. Parades always provide a bumper crop. You were just another bruised face with a busted lip, but then I saw Ms. Derouen's name mentioned in the overnights. Her name always gets my attention, you understand. She's become something of a hobby of mine." He leaned forward and added in a conspiratorial voice, "My colleagues consider my hobby more of an obsession. But what can you do? So I'm reading with more attention now, and I happened to see another name that gets my attention. Your name, Ash. I ask myself, 'How many Ashley Turners can there possibly be?' And, sure enough, it was you, the missing 'Ashley Turner' that I very much wanted to see. And here we are." The detective paused to take a small spiral notebook out of his shirt pocket. He flipped to a blank page and took out a pen, ready to write. "So that's my monologue on how I'm spending my years up to what is probably going to be mandatory early retirement. Now I want you to tell me, Ash, where have you been for the last year? What have you been up to?"

Ash felt like he was drowning again under the onslaught of words.

"Go on," the detective said, gesturing with his pen. "I'm

dying to hear it."

Ash thought of several possible responses. Then shook his head and offered, "I don't know."

The detective sighed. "Amnesia, Ash? Really? I can't write down 'amnesia'. That alone would probably force my early retirement all by itself. Come on, Ash. Your mother said you were a—" He paused to squint down at the paper in front of him. "A 'very bright boy'."

"I," Ash started. He tried to think of how to describe what was left of his memories, how he didn't even remember his mother, however bright she might think he was. "No. I just … don't know."

The detective stared at him. When he didn't offer anything else, the man said, "So tell me what you do remember."

"I," Ash started again. He shrugged and decided to go for it. "I was shot in the back of the head."

The detective's expression didn't change. "Go on."

"That's the last thing I remember," Ash said. He held his right hand up, thumb and forefinger extended like a pistol, and pointed it awkwardly at the back of his head. "I was shot in the back of the head." He pretended to pull the trigger when he said "shot". "By … I don't know their names. Would you like a description?"

The detective nodded. "Of course. First, though, when did this shooting occur?"

Ash took in a deep breath and let it out. "The night before Mardi Gras. Last year." He told about being taken by Big Man and Sneer.

"You were with Ms. Derouen at the time, yes?"

Ash reluctantly nodded. He hadn't mentioned her.

The detective made notes of the descriptions of Big Man and Sneer that Ash gave but didn't indicate whether the men sounded familiar. When Ash had finished his story, the detective asked, "And after that?"

"You believe me?"

The detective looked irritated at the question and tapped on his notebook. "I'm taking notes, Ash. What more do you want?" After a second, he added, "You do seem in remarkably good shape for having been executed gangster-style. But let's skip that for now. When do you start remembering again? After you were shot in the head?" He readied his pen.

"Last night." Ash told him about coming to in the water of the bayou, about the two poachers, Dewalt and Decker, and about seeing Jamie at the parade. Then about the man who gave him a ride into town when the detective asked about that.

"So," the detective said when Ash finished, "you remember nothing between being the time you were shot and last night?"

Ash shook his head. "Nothing."

"Well, Ash, that's not as helpful as I was hoping for." He held up the hand with the pen to forestall Ash's response. "Don't get me wrong, Ash. Your story about being abducted and shot does offer some interesting insights into the possible fates of these other young men. But ... amnesia? Really?"

"It's not just about last year," Ash said. "I ... There are holes in my memory. I can remember my father had lots of facial hair but was otherwise bald, but I can't remember anything about my mother. I can't remember my ex-wife's *name*, but I can remember she always wore rose-scented perfume. I can actually *smell* her perfume right now." He shifted in his seat. He started to pick up the cup of coffee again, but didn't. "But I can remember *everything* about Jamie. Everything. Down to the pores on her nose. And there's nothing ... No!" he almost shouted the word in response to the detective's expression. "There's no way she had anything to do with those other men. Big Man and Sneer worked for her father. She had nothing to do with it."

"She doesn't seem to have done a lot to stop it, Ash."

"No! She tried, but ..."

The detective smirked. "Did she look like was suffering when you saw her last night, Ash? Wearing widows weeds, maybe? No? Or was she was out with the same guy she had picked up last year, right before she picked up you." He nodded at Ash's expression of disbelief. "Oh, yes, Ms. Jamie Derouen has been a hobby of mine for some time, for far longer than you. I've made copious notes the last several years around this time. From what I observed of your behavior last year, Ash, and what happened last night, I would say you're at least as obsessed with her as I am. Though for completely different reasons. She was your rebound from a bad marriage. Me? I want her in jail, preferably on death row, awaiting lethal injection without anesthesia."

"It wasn't her!"

"You don't know anything, Ash."

"I know it wasn't her. It was her father. Those were his men, doing what he told them to do."

"You heard him give the order, did you?"

"No. I told you before. I only heard one side of the conversation."

"So I would say, in summation, that you don't know shit."

Ash pushed the coffee cup away from him and started to stand up. "I think we're done here—"

"Sit down, Ash. We aren't done. Unless you want to go back to the drunk tank? We can still arraign you for the drunk and disorderly, if that's what you want."

Ash settled back into his seat.

The detective leaned back and looked at Ash for a long minute. Finally, he said, "You're going to help me, Ash."

Ash shook his head. "No, I won't."

"So you're going to leave town, then? Never see Ms. Derouen again?"

Ash looked away.

"That's what I thought. You're even more obsessed now, I think, than you were last year."

Ash wanted to disagree, to say he wasn't obsessed. And maybe he hadn't been, then. Now, though, he seemed to be fixated on her. Even to himself he seemed ... *obsessed*.

"You were quite the dedicated private investigator last year," the detective said after a short pause. "You started with a chance meeting and only a first name and made it all the way to her front door and into her bed. No, don't get me wrong, Ash. I was impressed. You were quite the operator. And then I was just a little bit sad when you went missing the same way as all the others."

"It's not her. It's her father. He controls her life—"

"James Rémy Derouen controls a whole hell of a lot more in this city than just his daughter's life, Ash, let me assure you of that. In fact, it's Jamie Senior who has been nudging my superiors to nudge me into early retirement. If I can't wrap this up soon, one way or the other, my boss is going to agree with him. If there weren't fifteen verified missing tourists—and that last word is very important to a city like ours, Ash—I would already be gone. Retired. Maybe even buried somewhere." He paused. "I told you, Ash, you're a *tourist*. You come here and you think you know what's going on, but you haven't the first clue. You know a woman like Jamie Derouen two whole weeks and you think you know her soul, but you're a tourist there too. In and out and gone. You, my friend, don't know shit. And worse, you don't even know that you don't know. So you step in the shit and track it everywhere."

Ash met the man's eyes but said nothing. He tried to think a way out of this situation. But all he seemed to be able to think about was finding Jamie again. She had moved, but he had found her at the parade. That hadn't been all luck. And unlike last year, he knew her full name, and knew she was still in the city. He would find her.

"You really should just leave town, Ash," the detective said. "Your testimony wouldn't be worth shit if I put you on the stand, not with demonstrated head trauma and no evidence of assault. If I thought you'd get on the plane, I'd buy you a ticket home myself. But you wouldn't get on the plane, would you?"

Ash didn't answer.

The detective shrugged, then made a new stack of the manila folders. He took a large envelope from under the bottom of the stack. He tossed the envelope at Ash. "Your personal effects," he said. "What little there was. No ID, for instance. If Ms. Derouen hadn't identified you to the arresting officer, who knows how long you might have had to stay in the drunk tank."

Ash picked up the envelope. "You're not going to put me back in the drunk tank."

"Nope. Like I said, you're going to help me."

Ash shook his head. "No." He opened the envelope and dumped the contents on the table. A folded twenty dollar bill slid out along with leather cord strung through a set of yellowed animal teeth. "What's this?"

"Looks like alligator teeth to me. You were wearing it around your neck when you were brought in."

"Alligator teeth?"

"And maybe a few knucklebones. Authentic antiques, if you ask me. None of that tourist shit. So you don't remember this either?"

Ash shook his head. He was still looking at the teeth. They almost seemed alive, just waiting for something to bite down on.

"So you didn't buy that before your little headshot party in the swamp?"

"I don't know." Before he was sure what he would do with the necklace, his hands were lifting it over his head and settling it around his neck. He lowered his chin to his chest to look at the teeth. They still looked menacing. "I would never buy anything like this," he said, then moved the cord and teeth so they were out of sight. He picked up the twenty dollar bill and started to rise.

"Just one more minute, Ash. If you don't mind."

Ash sat back down.

The detective managed to look and sound concerned. Like the disappointed father figure in Ash's memories. He took a small, white card out of his shirt pocket and pushed it across the table to Ash.

"Take that, Ash. Keep it handy. It might save your life."

Ash picked up the card, but didn't read it. He pushed it into a pocket with the twenty dollar bill.

"I'm not the only person interested in you, Ash," the detective went on. "You know that, don't you? You stay here, in jail, you're probably safe. For a day or two. But you walk out of here, and those other interested parties are going to want to speak to you. And you may not like what they have to say either."

"I'll take my chances."

The detective smiled, all traces of concern evaporating. The mustache took on a menacing upward curve. "That you will, and so will I. One way or the other, Ash, you're going to help me. Whether you want to or not." He paused. "Do you know how we trap alligators around here, Ash?" He didn't wait for Ash to respond. "There's a lot of ways, I guess, but all of them include one primary ingredient."

"Chicken?" The memory from his first swamp tour, the one that hadn't ended so badly, bubbled up from the murk of Ash's mind.

The detective snorted a quick chuckle. "Among other things. All of those things being bait, Ash. Tender, juicy bait hung up on a hook and left where the gators can see it. And get to it." He extended his arm as if there were a piece of chicken hanging by a string from his fingertips. "Right on top of the water. Gators like their dead meat to marinate just a bit."

"So if I don't help you, I'm bait?"

"You're bait whether you help me or not, Ash. Live bait, hanging there, marinating while we wait. The question is whether you're still living when the trap is checked."

Ash pushed his chair back and stood. He waited for the detective to say something else. When he didn't, Ash left the interrogation room. Then, when no one stopped him, he made his way out of the police station.

He needed to find Jamie.

Ash splashed water on his face. The smell of chlorine stung his nostrils, and he detected hints of other chemicals that he didn't have names for. Still, he enjoyed the cool feel of the water on his skin so much that he did it again. Then again. Then several more times, dragging his wet fingers through his hair. Then once more because he knew he wouldn't be able to do it again for a while.

He straightened and looked at his face in the dusty mirror. His short hair had not been slicked back by the water so much as encouraged to stick out in clumps. At least he no longer looked quite so much like he had spent the night in the drunk tank. He wrinkled his nose when he realized he still smelled as if he had. He wondered when he might have a chance to take a shower again. He thought of the small hotel where he had stayed, then realized they would not want to see him again. He had extended his stay a year ago, then disappeared before paying the bill. No, he would have to find some other place.

Still looking in the mirror, he noticed a scattering of tiny bumps that traced the line of his jaw, just visible beneath the stubble of his beard. Both sides of his jaw, he saw. The bumps all sported tiny black spots, like some kind of acne. Had there been something in the swamp water that aggravated his skin? Or something he had eaten—?

At the thought of food, his stomach woke up. With a low growl, his stomach pointed out that he could not remember eating anything in over a year. The fried food smells—especially the oysters—that had almost turned his stomach when he walked into the restaurant now enticed him.

A knock on the hollow wooden door of the tiny bathroom startled him.

"Occupied," Ash said.

"I know," said a man's voice outside the door. "That's why I knocked."

"Just a minute."

Ash started to turn away from his reflection, but stopped when he saw something red in his right eye. He leaned forward again to get a closer look. He shifted his attention from his right eye to his left eye and back. His eyes weren't especially bloodshot, just tired-looking, with bags underneath. He caught the red flash again as he moved his head back. He glanced up at the green-ish flourescent lights above the mirror, then back at his eyes. At just the right angle, his black pupils became red dots in the middle of his irises.

Had they always done that?

The man knocked on the door again.

Ash slid the dead bolt back on the door and stepped out. He nodded to the man standing there, then pushed past him back into the dim, narrow dining room.

There were a few more people eating early lunches than when he had first arrived. He sat down on one of the cracked-vinyl stools along the bar. Behind the bar, a black man wearing a white apron was applying the finishing touches to a classic po-boy sandwich. A loaf of French bread nearly a yard long had been split in two and piled high with fried shrimp and fried oysters.

The black man met Ash's eye, gave him an incline nod of greeting, then carefully placed the top half of the loaf of bread on the sandwich. He eyed the sandwich as if to insure no imperfections, then picked up a long serrated knife. He positioned the knife over the middle of the sandwich. As he sawed through the thick sandwich, he asked Ash, "What you have?"

Ash managed a smile. "I was going to ask you the same thing, but my question is already answered." He retrieved the twenty dollar bill from his pocket, then held it up so the man could see it. He laid it on the bar. "How much of that marvelous po-boy can a man buy with this? And a beer?"

The black man smiled. "I think we can fill you up. Maybe even leave you a bit of change for a side of some much-needed aspirin." He finished cutting the sandwich in half, then cut the two halves into quarters.

"I look that bad?"

The man shrugged. "You look better than when I saw you walk out of the PD." He nodded in the direction of the police station visible through the big front window. "Looked like a fun crowd you was with last night. Must have been some party. Or maybe they're throwing hungry gators out the floats these days?" He gestured to the tears in Ash's shirt.

Ash looked down at his ruined shirt. "No gators," he said. Then added, "That I recall. But, no, it wasn't fun at all."

"Then you'll definitely be wanting that side of aspirin."

7

FEELING SATED BY food, and warmed by a beer and a few laughs, Ash stepped out of the cave-like diner and into the wan February sunshine.

"You find your woman," Darrel said, "and you bring her back here. I always wanted to meet Helen of Troy, and she sounds about as close as I'll ever get."

The cook had laughed, shaken Ash's hand and introduced himself as Darrel when Ash finished the first half of the po-boy sandwich, one quarter after the next, and asked for the next section. "You can really pack it away for a skinny white boy. No offense."

"None taken." Ash had been as surprised as Darrel. He had been certain the first quarter of the huge sandwich would have been sufficient. By the time Ash had started on the final quarter, the lunch crowd had filled the restaurant, and more than a few of them crowded Ash at the bar, watching him eat.

"Getting ready for Mardi Gras, are you?" Darrel asked as he worked on more sandwiches. "Giving up po-boys for Lent? Or are you some kind of competitive eater. Like that guy on TV, goes around eating everything in sight?"

"Just," Ash said between bites, "really ... hungry ... Today."

When Ash had swallowed the last bite of the final quarter of the po-boy, Darrel had shaken his head. He pushed the twenty dollar bill back to Ash. "You keep your money, man. Like my momma used to say, does a cook good to see someone eat like that once in a while. But next time," he added with a smile, "you'll be paying. Only one freebie per glutton is my policy."

More than one person patted him on the back or punched him in the shoulder on his way out of the restaurant, congratulating him. Unsure what else to say, Ash had mumbled thanks and tried to smile back.

Outside on the sidewalk the sunlight was filtered by a low haze that threatened to become gray clouds at any minute, but Ash didn't mind. Any sunlight seemed like a treat, and added energy with every step.

Now that he was fed and warm again, he found he could push his need to find Jamie to one side and consider *why* he needed to find her so bad. Especially after everything the detective had told him.

He had been infatuated, definitely. He had bordered on—probably even stepped over the line into—stalking in his initial search for a woman he had seen less than a minute and knew only as "Jamie". But she had seemed to welcome his attentions, smiling at him when he had found her again at each parade, even though she had been with Frank, the ignorable man, every time. Each time, of course, the ignorable man had become angrier and angrier, until he had stomped out of the picture entirely. Then Ash had been free to tell her his name wasn't Marcus, and she had smiled and told him, *Of course it isn't. But I needed a name for you. You never gave me one.*

The memory of Jamie's smile made him smile. Then his smiled faltered.

Had Jamie known what was going to happen? Is that why she had told him to call *after* Mardi Gras? She had tried to help him that night. She had even tried to call her father—

His memories raced forward, through the abduction and the drive and the sudden, painful conclusion. Had he really been shot? His right hand found its way to the back of his head. His fingers searched his scalp for any sign of a scar where the bullet must have entered. He found nothing. He forced himself to return his hand to his side and pushed the question of the shooting to one side.

Where had he been for a year? What was he not remembering?

He didn't notice the black minivan until it pulled up next to him and came to a full stop.

He was still turning to look at the minivan when the side door clicked open and slid back. Two men wearing thick-framed sunglasses and dark suits stepped out of the minivan. They were dressed identically, but one of the men was a full twelve inches taller than the other, and at least six inches taller than Ash.

"Come with us, Mr. Turner," said the shorter man. "You have a date. Again." His voice and the lopsided sneer on his face were instantly familiar. *Come on, asshole. You have a date.* Sneer grabbed Ash's left arm and pulled him toward the van as Big Man took position behind him, pushing.

Ash pulled his arm back. "No, I'm not going anywhere." He looked up and down the street to see if anyone had noticed what was happening. And to find an escape route—

He heard the crackle of the taser less than a second before the powerful charge hit him in the back. His neck froze in mid-turn and the muscles of his left arm siezed and clenched, hitting him in the chest with his own fist. Every muscle in his body tried to do whatever it had been doing at full capacity. The pain as the muscles fought against each other and their attachments to his bones hit all at once. He expected to black out from the pain, but didn't. So he was conscious, but helpless, as the men pushed him into the van, lifted him into a captain's seat behind the front passenger's seat, then zip tied his arms to the arm rests. Big Man took the seat next to him. Sneer pulled the van door closed, then stepped around Ash to sit in the back. The vehicle lurched into motion.

When he could move again, Ash tugged against the zip ties, but they were too tight. The plastic straps dug into the flesh of his forearms. He couldn't even pull his arms back far enough to relieve some of the pressure.

Big Man turned to look at Ash.

"Remember me, Mr. Turner?" He took off his sunglasses as if to be certain Ash recognized him. "I'll bet you never thought you'd see us—"

Sneer's face appeared next to Ash, cutting off his view of Big Man. Sneer did what he did best as he stuffed a rubber gag into Ash's mouth. "Remember me too, Mr. Turner?" He pressed his index finger against Ash's temple. "Boom!" he shouted, rocking Ash's head sideways.

"Maybe it'll actually work this time—" Big Man said.

"It worked last time, damn it," Sneer said as he moved backward again and out of Ash's view. "You saw it too. This fucker is a dead man walking. One way or the other."

The minivan drove past the police station as they sped away. The detective stood outside the front doors, smoking a cigarette. The man's eyes followed the progress of the minivan and Ash wonderd if the man could see him. He found himself thinking about alligator bait.

8

HIS ABDUCTORS DID not cover his head. They made no attempt to hide where they were taking Ash. They drove through the city's downtown, then along streets Ash had never seen, finally turning into a rundown neighborhood with few cars. The minivan pulled into the covered driveway of single-story home that looked like it hadn't been lived in for a decade or more. The door facing the carport had been painted more recently than the rest of the house, but beneath the fading layer of new paint could be seen the spray painted X-code added after Hurricane Katrina. Beyond the car port, the swamp had begun to reclaim the overgrown backyard.

Ash was surprised at how calm he was. Not panicking. A year ago when almost the exact same thing had happened, he had spent the trip talking as fast as he could, trying to talk the men out of doing what they claimed they weren't doing and so clearly were. It had been all he could do to keep his bowels under control when Big Man had steered the SUV off the road and onto a dark dirt road overhung with drooping branches. This time, though, Ash found he was sitting quietly, ignoring the jibes and questions of the four men in the minivan with him. He was as scared now as he had been then, he just wasn't about to shit himself and seemed able to keep his fear bottled up, out of the way of his mind's constant search for a way out. Any opportunity that might present itself. He decided he liked this approach to the situation much better.

The neighborhood looked too deserted for there to be anyone who might help him. The urbanized wilderness of the swamp behind the house, though, looked like refuge. If he could run into that like he had run away from Dewalt and Decker he might have a chance.

Something tickled the back of his mind as he looked at the vine-tangled tree branches and he felt the eyes of the bayou on him again. Looking out of the swamp at him.

Danger waited for him in the swamp. He could feel it. A thirst for blood. A need to grip and tear. A need for vengeance as great as Ash's need to find Jamie.

Ash felt himself shrinking from that unseen gaze. But he had survived the swamp once already. Maybe twice. He doubted he would survive whatever Big Man and Sneer had in mind for him.

As soon as the minivan had parked, the driver got out and came around to the side of the van. Big Man opened the driver's side sliding door and stepped out. He pulled that door closed tight, then walked around to join the driver. He took out his taser as the driver opened the door. Sneer came from the back and bent over Ash.

Ash bunched his muscles as he watched Sneer pull a large folding knife out a pocket and snap the blade into position. Sneer noticed and his sneer became a lopsided smile as he leaned closer. "Feeling helpless, Mr. Turner?" His breath on Ash's face stank of raw oysters, garlic, and alcohol. "Don't you worry. I'll be real gentle." With two deft flicks of his wrist he cut the zip ties securing Ash's arms. Then he waved the blade in front of Ash's face.

Grabbing Sneer's knife arm with both hands, Ash held the blade away from his face as he pushed himself out of the chair and into Sneer, pushing them both out of the van. They fell in a tangle of arms. Sneer hit the ground on his back and let out a painful grunt. Ash lost track of the knife as he fought to free himself from Sneer's stunned grip. He made it to his feet, with Sneer on the ground beneath him. Then Big Man stepped up and gave him another jolt of the taser. He crumpled in a spasm of pain.

Big Man looked down at Ash. "You should be more cooperative, Mr. Turner—"

"Fucker!" Sneer shouted, shoving Ash's body away from him. He got to his feet and kicked Ash in the gut hard enough to threaten Ash's huge lunch. "Motherfucker!" He kicked Ash again.

"That's enough—"

"I'll kick him as many times as I want." Sneer kicked Ash again. He pulled back his leg as if to kick Ash again, then stepped back. "But that will do. For now. Get up, asshole."

Breathing was pain. Breathing made him cough and gag, and both of those caused even more pain. Ash wondered if he had a broken rib. He pushed himself to his hands and knees. Before he could get to his feet, though, the driver and another man Ash hadn't seen grabbed him by the arms. The fourth man, the one holding Ash's left arm, wasn't wearing a suit. He was dressed in drab green cargo pants and a black sleeveless undershirt. The two men dragged him toward the now-open door of the house.

Sneer stood ready with his recovered knife while Big Man watched the streets and houses as the two men dragged Ash into the house.

The house was as rundown on the inside as the outside and smelled as bad as the drunk tank. The combined living room and dining room had only a few folding chairs, one of them propping up a small flatscreen TV near a wall. Empty pizza boxes, Asian takeout cartons, and fast food drive-thru bags filled the corner where a small dining table should have been.

The men dragged Ash through the living room, down a short hall and into what had once been a bedroom. There was only one window in the room, barred on the outside, dirty inside and out, that faced the swamp in the back. Indirect sunlight came through the dusty Venetian blinds and illuminated a workbench that had been built at an angle. Leather straps hung from the workbench, and a large plastic basin rested beneath the low end. A cheap plastic folding table with rusted metal legs had been pushed against one wall along with a folded step stool and an overflowing trash can.

"Up you go," said Driver, still pulling on Ash's right arm. They dragged Ash toward the workbench.

The effects of the taser were wearing off, allowing Ash to struggle. He pulled at his arms and tried to get his feet underneath him. Until Big Man tasered him again.

"God damn it!" shouted Driver as Ash fell painfully to the floor and twitched on the moldy carpet. "I was still holding him."

Sneer laughed.

"And you didn't feel a thing, did you, you big baby," Big Man said. "Now get him up there."

"The hell I 'didn't feel a thing'," Driver said. "Made my hair stand on end."

"I didn't feel anything," said Left Arm.

"How many charges you got in that thing?" Driver asked.

"Stop whining—" Big Man started.

"Get him on the fucking platform," Sneer said.

"I wish you would stop interrupting—."

"Fuck you."

Ash managed to swing his right arm to ward off Driver. He kicked weakly at Left Arm.

"God damn it, you two," Big Man said. "Do I need to tie him up for you too? Help them," he added, nodding to Sneer.

"Fuck you," Sneer said again, but he helped Driver and Left Arm pick Ash up off the floor and drop him on the workbench, head on the low end. Then Big Man held the arcing taser in front of Ash's face while the leather straps were pulled tight across Ash's legs, torso, and chest. Ash's arms were secured beneath the straps that held his chest and torso. A final strap went over Ash's knees, tight enough to threaten the joints with hyperextension.

Sneer knocked Big Man's hand away and leaned close to Ash's face. "Feeling helpless now, Mr. Turner?"

Before he had fully thought of it, Ash jerked his head forward and snapped his teeth at Sneer's nose.

Sneer jerked back. When the other men laughed, Sneer balled his right fist and hit Ash on the side of the head. The impact knocked Ash's head hard enough to pop his neck. His eyes struggled to regain focus as his head lolled back to a more normal position. He took a breath to spit in Sneer's face, but the effort awoke the pain in his ribs and he choked instead.

Big Man, still holding the taser but no longer arcing it, leaned over Ash from the opposite side. "We're in a lot of trouble because of you, Mr. Turner. Did you know—?"

"That's right, dumbass," Sneer said, then hit Ash again. "Because you don't have the fucking *sense* to stay fucking *dead*, we have this unnecessary drama."

"We would like to know where you've been the past year. Who helped you?"

"I don't know," Ash said. "But even if I did know—"

Sneer hit him again. Ash's ear felt as if it had busted.

"Still handing out that amnesia line?"

Ash forced his eyes to focus on Big Man. "How did you—?"

This time Sneer's fist hit him on the left cheek, just below the eye.

"Hey," said Left Arm. "Leave something for me."

Sneer pulled his fist back, but Big Man held up a hand. "Stop, damn it. You break his jaw and he's not going to be able to tell us anything—"

Sneer brought his fist down on Ash's chest almost as hard as he had kicked Ash before. Ash grunted in pain, then gasped for breath.

"Feel better?" Big Man asked.

"No," Sneer said.

"Too fucking bad. We got to go." To Ash, he added, "Enjoy your stay, Mr. Turner. We'll be bringing you back some company for your body bag."

"I thought ... you weren't going ... to kill me ...?"

Sneer laughed.

Big Man chuckled and shook his head. "Not yet, no. We got some questions to ask you first—"

"Fuck you guys," Left Arm said. "If either of you knew the first thing about proper enhanced interrogation techniques—"

"Don't fucking interrupt me," Big Man said.

"You don't tell the subject you're going to kill him anyway—"

"Don't," Big Man said. "Fucking." He no longer held the taser. He had put it away and drawn a black pistol almost instantaneously. He held the gun down at his side. "Interrupt. Me."

"Sorry," Left Arm said, holding his hands up and backing away from Big Man.

"And have more faith in yourself." Big Man put the pistol away, then smiled again. "He'll talk. Won't you, Mr. Turner? Just watch him till we—"

"Feel free to scream for help as much as you want," Sneer said as he leaned over Ash again. Ash flinched as Sneer drew back a hand, then only patted Ash on the cheek. "No one lives in this neighborhood any more, so no one but Johnny will hear you. Which is OK, because Johnny likes it."

"Fuck you," Left Arm Johnny protested. "I don't *like* it. I'm just doing my job—"

"Shut up, both of you," Big Man said. "Come on."

Sneer patted Ash on the cheek one more time, then he and Big Man left the room. Ash heard them walk through the living room, call out for the driver, then the three of them left.

"Just make yourself comfortable, Mr. Turner," Left Arm Johnny said. "And forget what that asshole said about screaming. You start screaming and ... well. You won't like it. You just lay there all relaxing and shit and I'll turn up the TV so you can hear it."

LEFT ARM JOHNNY left Ash alone in the room. Ash heard the man turn on the TV, then rifle through the heap of takeout bags and boxes looking for something to eat.

Ash looked around the room he was in. The room had obviously been a girl's bedroom at one point. A faded movie poster for *The Princess and Frog* adorned one wall, hanging at a rumpled angle from its last thumbtack, the lowest corner torn and curling up. Once-bright stickers of flowers, butterflies, and cartoon characters that Ash didn't recognize also adorned the walls, most of them about eye-level for a six-year-old. Whatever furniture the little girl had had, though, was gone, except the dented, pink wire mesh trash can in the corner near Ash's head. Like the living room, the trash can had fast food wrappers and bags, but also snips of wire, some of it of heavy gauge, like that used for jumper cables.

He saw the rest of the jumper cables hung from the ceiling. Holes had been punched through the sheetrock so the heavy wires could be tied around a ceiling joist. The wires hung down about two feet and ended in steel-reinforched leather shackles that had probably been sex toys in a previous life. Ash twisted his head and saw stains on the carpet below the shackles. He could smell the dried blood, urine and shit, as well as the bleach that had not been used properly during the clean up and had left negative stains of its own.

Once again, Ash was amazed at his lack of a emotional response. He could feel, deep down, the fear, but it didn't touch him the way it should have. His heart rate and his breathing remained steady. The fear was there, but it was as if he were observing someone else experiencing it. The way Big Man and Sneer had watched Jamie crying and Ash shakily getting dressed—

Thoughts of Jamie provoked a reaction. He had to find Jamie. He had to escape. Not to save his own life from the torture he knew was coming, but to find Jamie.

Ash tried to twist against of the leather straps, but they were too tight.

"Settle down in there," Left Arm Johnny shouted when Ash let out a grunt of frustrated effort.

"I have to find her!"

"I'm not kidding, man."

Ash clamped his jaw shut. His need for Jamie burned in his brain, forcing him to push and twist against his bonds. He needed to find Jamie, to hold her—

His hands clenched as if they were grabbing Jamie's shoulders and holding her.

His mouth opened wide—wider than it should have, causing a popping sound and a stab of pain in the joints of his jaw that startled him.

The muscles of his arms tensed and bulged as if he were pulling Jamie to him, and into his gaping mouth. His jaw clamped shut, hard, on empty air.

The pain of his teeth coming together, combined with his own confusion and an explosion of the fear he had thought so well contained, caused him to cry out. He shouted words he didn't understand. Or maybe they weren't words at all, only primal sounds from a part of him that he had never known he possessed.

"Don't make me come in there."

Trembling, his breaths coming fast, feeling almost as if he had been hit with Big Man's taser again, Ash stared at the cracks and cobwebs where the wall and ceiling came together, wondering what the hell had just happened.

His life had offered him few convictions, few beliefs as absolute as his need to find Jamie.

But needed her for ... what?

His lips pulled back from his teeth, but he refused to allow his mouth to open. He couldn't stop his hands from clenching and unclenching, futilely grabbing for—

He didn't want to think about what he might be grabbing for.

In the living room, Left Arm Johnny changed the channel to a sports talk show, then turned the volume way up. The voices of the arguing men ramped up to a level that made Ash wonder if Left Arm Johnny was going deaf. He could still hear the man moving around in the living room and kitchen, but couldn't make out what was happening because of the TV.

"That's better," Left Arm Johnny said from the door after a few minutes. "Stay calm like that. Relaxed."

Ash twisted his head to glare at Left Arm Johnny. He started to say that he was not calm, nor relaxed, but he stopped when he saw the large roll of plastic sheeting under the man's arm. Left Arm Johnny had a butcher's apron on that covered him from chest to knees, and wore big plastic gloves.

"I have some work I need to do in the next room, so don't think I've gone anywhere. I can still hear you." He started to move away from the door, but stopped. "Is the TV loud enough?" he asked.

After a few seconds, Ash managed a shrug.

Left Arm Johnny smiled. "It is? Good."

When Left Arm Johnny was gone, Ash found himself looking at the one dirty window. His vantage point was so close to the floor he could see only a the tops of the trees that grew from the encroaching swamp, and the gray sky above their branches. But he could still feel the eyes of the bayou out there. Watching. Waiting.

10

ASH IGNORED THE TV show talkers and their predictions for the last few weeks of the NBA season and playoffs. Left Arm Johnny had gone back and forth past the door of his room several times, then started working in the next bedroom. Ash heard the rustling sounds of plastic sheeting being spread on the floor, then the long tearing sounds of duct tape.

Ash tried not to think about why—or who—the preparations were for. But following Left Arm Johnny's progress did provide a distraction from his own confused thoughts about Jamie.

Every time he thought of her name, his fingers twitched. Sometimes he bared his teeth.

Had the detective's information about her influenced him? Had seeing her with the Ignorable Man made him angrier than he suspected? Maybe when Frank had hit him? None of these thoughts drew any reaction from his subsconscious. The part of him that needed her offered no hints, only physical ticks with more than a hint of violence. Maybe it was all the blood pooling in his head from being strapped head down on the slanted workbench.

While he listened to Left Arm Johnny working in the next room and tried to sort his feelings-ugres-needs concerning Jamie Derouen, he continued to struggle against the leather straps that held him.

He managed to twist his right leg. This reduced the pressure on his right knee and ankle, but seemed to increase the pressure on his hips. When he tried to twist his leg back to its original position, the leather straps refused to stretch.

By nearly hyperextending his right elbow, he was able to pull his right hand free of the strap that pressed against his hips. Doing the same thing to his left arm freed that hand, as well. He felt along the straps where he could but found nothing his fingers could untie or unbuckle.

He raised his head as much as he could, pushing his chin into his chest, but saw nothing he could exploit. When the strain in his neck became too much, he settled back with a disappointed sigh that came out more like a low growl.

"Yeah," said Left Arm Johnny from the door. "It's like I've done this sort of thing before."

Startled, Ash's body jerked.

Left Army Johnny laughed. He still had on the butcher's apron, but his hands were empty. He pointed at Ash. "I love it when that happens. People get so *focused* sometimes, you can just sneak up on them." He crossed his arms and leaned against the doorframe. "But, yeah, you tie enough people to a plank, you'll figure out how to do it right. I made that myself," he added, nodding at Ash and the slanted workbench. "She's not much to look at it, but she's one hundred percent functional." He opened his mouth to say something else, then cocked his head as he heard the same thing Ash did.

The minivan had returned.

"Oh, good. They're back." Left Arm Johnny smiled and uncrossed his arms as he stood straight again. He pointed a finger at Ash. "You stay there, OK? We'll get started in a few minutes."

11

"IN YOU GO, tough guy," Sneer said as he and Driver pushed a struggling man into the room with Ash. The man wore what Ash thought of as "vacation casual". Pleated charcoal trousers and a Polo shirt. He had on only one loafer, the other probably lost during the rough trip from the minivan that Ash had overheard.

The man's eyes met Ash's. "Marcus?"

"Frank?"

The Ignorable Man looked frightened, his face pale, his eyes taking in Ash belted to the workbench, then the wires hanging from the ceiling.

"What's going on, Marcus? Who are these men?"

Ash considered several responses, and chose, "My name isn't Marcus. You *know* my name isn't Marcus." The same words he had spoken to Jamie a year ago. He wondered if the Ignorable Man spotted the irony.

Frank just stared at him.

Sneer pushed Frank from behind and sent the man stumbling past Ash, into a corner. "I knew it! I was sure you two knew each other. Banging the same woman, and all."

Frank turned around to face everyone in the room, his back to the corner. He looked at Ash, then at the barred window, then at Sneer and Big Man. Behind them, Left Arm Johnny stood in the door, still wearing the butcher's apron.

Instead of his taser, Big Man held his automatic pistol. He gestured to both Ash and Frank with the pistol. "This year, meet last year. Last year, meet this—"

"Ha!" Sneer guffawed loudly. "That's rich."

"I'm talking here," Big Man said. Sneer rolled his eyes, but contained himself to a low chuckle. Big Man went on, "Mr. Largent, meet Mr. Turner. I expect you remember Mr. Turner, since he took your place last year. In more ways than one."

"What do you want? I can pay—"

Big Man pointed his pistol at Frank's face. "I said I'm *fucking talking* here."

Frank pulled back into the corner as if he had been struck. His eyes were moving nonstop, trying to see all the threats that confronted him when they weren't begging Ash to help him. Ash met the man's gaze, but he had no help to offer. Frank slid down the wall until he was sitting with his knees pulled to his chest.

"You should thank him, Mr. Largent. Mr. Turner here took your place last year. He gave you one extra year of life. I hope you spent it well. Maybe made yourself a bucket list—"

"Cause now you're going to kick that bucket," Sneer said.

Big Man glared at Sneer, then went on. "So I think you should say 'thank you' to Mr. Turner."

Frank seized the pause. "You work for Jamie's father, right?" he asked, talking fast. "If you just want me to leave Jamie alone, I can do that. You'll never see me again. I won't even come back to Louisiana again. Hell, you can have the whole Gulf coast—"

"Don't!" Ash shouted when he saw Big Man's trigger finger tense. He thought he heard Left Arm Johnny shouting the same thing.

Big Man ignored all of them. The shot echoed in the small room, the sound like a pair of hammers slamming into Ash's eardrums.

The bullet hit Frank's forehead just above the left eye. Blood, brain and bits of skull sprayed into the corner behind the man and painted the dingy walls. After a few heartbeats that seemed to stretch into minutes, the shocked expression on Frank's face relaxed and he fell to his left.

"God damn it!" Left Arm Johnny shouted. He pointed in the direction of the next room. "I had the room all prepared, just like you asked. Fuck, man. Are you going to clean that up?"

Big Man turned to face Left Arm Johnny. He tucked his pistol back into its holster under his jacket. He smiled at Left Arm Johnny, then turned to speak to Sneer over his shoulder. "Check his pulse."

"Check his pulse?" Sneer asked. "His fucking *brains* are all over the fucking *wall*."

"Yes, check his pulse. The Boss was very specific on this point. We shoot him, then we check his pulse and making sure he's fucking dead this time."

"He," Sneer said, pointing at Ash, "was dead last time. You know it. I know it. The fucking *gators* knew it."

"Check his pulse."

"You're not going to clean that up, are you?" Left Arm Johnny asked.

Big Man continued to ignore Left Arm Johnny. He watched Sneer kneel down by the body of Frank and press two fingers on Frank's neck.

"Oh my god," Sneer said, eyes unnaturally wide with surprise and sarcasm thick in his voice. "He's dead." He removed his fingers and stood.

"Good to hear," Big Man said. He looked at Left Arm Johnny. "Now it's your turn. Get that in your butcher shop and take care—"

"Save me a drumstick," Sneer said. "I love drumsticks."

"Give me a hand," Left Arm Johnny said to Sneer.

Sneer shook his head. "Fuck no. I just got this suit dry-cleaned." He adjusted the lapels of his jacket. "I think I saw a gator out back," he added, turning to peer out the dirty window. "Can we feed these assholes to him? Save ourselves the trip?"

Big Man shook his head. "Don't be a dumbass."

Big Man and Sneer stood on opposite sides of Ash's head as Left Arm Johnny pulled Frank's body away from the wall enough to step behind it. Then he squatted down, hooked his hands under Frank's arms, and stood. He dragged the body out of the room, muttering under his breath.

"I prepared the fucking room, fucker, just like you asked. Then you shoot him in here."

If Big Man heard, he said nothing. He looked down at Ash. "Don't worry, Mr. Turner. He'll be back for—"

"I'll make sure he brings you a wing," Sneer said. "You like wings, right?"

12

LEFT ARM JOHNNY was no longer wearing the butcher's apron when he came back into the room. Instead he wore waders that covered him to the chest. A worn, yellow bath towel hung around his neck, and he carried two plastic milk jugs full of water. He saw Ash's look and gave him a winning smile.

"Did you think I had forgotten about you?"

"What are you doing?" Ash asked.

Left Arm Johnny just smiled wider. He placed the jugs on the folding table near the wall, then pulled the table out until it was parallel to the workbench. Ash's head was below the level of the jugs. Left Arm Johnny left the room and came back with two more full jugs. Then two more. He arranged the jugs in neat ranks of two on the table. He walked over to where the step stool leaned against the wall and picked it up. He unfolded the step stool and placed it next to the bench opposite the table.

He went to the door of the room and shouted, "I'm about to start."

"About time—" Big Man started to say.

"Keep it down," Sneer shouted back. "I'm trying to

71

watch TV."

"Assholes," Left Arm Johnny muttered. He turned to face Ash again. "Fine. Let's get started."

Ash looked away and stared at the barred window. He heard Left Arm Johnny come around the workbench. The man came into view and put a foot on the first step of the stool. Ash turned his head away again, to look at the door to the bedroom.

"Look at me, Mr. Turner."

"Stop calling me that," Ash said to the empty doorframe. "My name is Ash."

"OK. Look at me, *Ash*."

Ash turned back to face the man.

"Do you want to tell me where you've been the last year, Ash? Try to prevent a lot of ugliness?"

Ash sighed. "I would tell you if I knew."

Left Arm Johnny smiled his winning smile again. "Good. I am so glad you said that." He brought his other foot up to the second step of the stool. He loomed over Ash, still smiling. With his left hand, he whipped the towel from around his neck and dropped it on Ash's face. The towel hung low on both sides of Ash's face. Ash twisted his head back and forth but couldn't shake it loose.

Then the heavy weight of Left Arm Johnny landed on his chest and he gasped for breath as the man straddled him.

"If you don't mind," Left Arm Johnny said, his voice slighlty muffled by the towel, "don't try to talk right now. I like to do this in a very structured way. First, I ask you the question. Then, you answer. Or you don't. Or maybe you answer and I don't like that answer. Either way, you get wet. Then we do it again. So, please, if you don't mind, wait until I ask you again before blurting out what I want to know." Ash felt the man lean over and pick up a jug from the table beside the work bench. "And we're off!"

Cold water splashed against the towel on Ash's face and the fabric quickly became soaked. Left Arm Johnny's weight shifted and more water hit the towel. This time it was as if the towel wasn't even there and the water was splashing directly on his face. Ash kept his mouth closed, but water poured into his nostrils and down his throat. He was forced to open his mouth to cough. He tried to spit out the water, but more poured through the towel and into both his mouth and nose. He felt water soaking his hair and dripping into his ears. The sound of the plastic jug glug-glug-glugging its contents sounded like his own choked retching.

Unable to move his arms or legs or any other part of his body, claustrophobia closed in on Ash, squeezing the towel even tighter to his face and around his neck. His attempts to spit out the water failed, and he gagged and nearly vomited. He wanted to take a breath, to force himself to calm down, but there was no way to breathe without sucking in water.

An inexplicably calm portion of his mind noted that the water was just tap water. A taste of rust from old pipes and plastic from the jug, a hint of chlorine and laundry detergent—probably from the towel—but no dirt, no fish, no bugs. A fresh glug-douse of water washed away most of the bile that he had failed to push through the wet towel.

"OK," Left Arm Johnny said. "That was the first course. And I think you took it like a champ. You get full credit for that one, Ash."

Ash gasped, expelling the stale air in his lungs, then took in a quick breath. He almost choked as his attempted breath pulled the wet towel into his mouth. He could barely pull air through the heavy, wet cloth, especially with the man sitting on his chest.

"Sorry about that, Ash." The wet towel was peeled

away from Ash's face and out of his mouth. "Don't want you choking to death."

Ash panted, ignoring the water that still irritated his nasal cavaties and lungs.

Left Arm Johnny was smiling down at Ash. His rubber-sleeved legs dangled to either side. "So let's try that again, shall we? Pay attention, Ash. Here are the questions." He paused. "Where have you been the last year, Ash? Who helped you?"

"I ... don't," Ash started. "Wait!" he added as the man's smile became a frown. "Please. Wait." He struggled to breathe, while trying to take as many breaths as he could. As if breaths could be stored up and saved somehow. "What do you want to know? How can I convince you that I don't remember anything?"

Left Arm Johnny shook his head. "Ash, Ash, Ash. I've been very clear about what I want to know. As for convincing me, I'd like to think I've been very clear about that too."

Ash took a deep breath as Left Arm Johnny positioned the wet towel over his face.

The man held the towel over his face, smiling again. Waiting.

Ash let the breath out. "What?"

The towel dropped into place.

Left Arm Johnny laughed as Ash tried to suck in a new breath against the weight of the towel. Ash shook his head back and forth, but the wet fabric clung to his face.

"Give me a second, will you, Ash?"

Ash felt Left Arm Johnny swing a leg over his head, then step down. The weight lifting off Ash's chest felt good, but he could still pull only the most limited amount of air through the wet towel. He sucked at the towel, drawing in the water. He swallowed and tried again. The ratio of water to air improved.

"You *are* a quick one, Ash."

Ash continued to try and pull as much air through the towel as he could as Left Arm Johnny climbed heavily up the step stool, then settled on Ash's chest.

"Now let's try this again."

That was all the warning Ash got before the new jug of water started glugging and splashing water on his face. He resisted the urge to try and take a last breath, and just closed his mouth and eyes tight as the water coursed over his face.

Somehow, no water went up his nose. He could only think it was because he wasn't breathing. Except the angle of the workbench should have let gravity at least dribble water in.

"Come on, Ash," Left Arm Johnny said. "No cheating." The man's legs flexed, the weight on Ash's chest lifted, then came crashing back down.

The held breath sputtered out of Ash, causing the towel to balloon away from his face briefly. Then the jug-glugging flow of water resumed and the towel was there again, the water pushing it into his mouth as he choked and gagged. Ash struggled not to breathe in water as he choked, but still no water went up his nose.

The water stopped. Left Arm Johnny dropped the empty jug to the floor, but didn't remove the towel from Ash's face. Ash sucked against the wet terrycloth, seeking air. It couldn't have been more than twenty or thirty seconds before Left Arm Johnny peeled back the towel, but it seemed an eternity. Ash was lightheaded from the effort of breathing and the limited air he was getting. The blood pooling in his head seemed to slosh as his heart pounded in his chest.

"Why did you come back, Ash? Who sent you—?"

"I need ... to find ... Jamie," Ash said, gasping as he tried to talk, answering the first question before he knew what he was doing. Not because of the torture, though. Because the man had finally asked a question Ash could answer. His fingers had clenched as he answered. He left them that way.

Left Arm Johnny nodded. "Fair enough. And … ?"

Ash just stared at him, blinking against the water that dripped into his eyes.

The man gestured with his right hand, twirling it around as if prompting a child.

"I don't—" He stopped when Left Arm Johnny let out a deep, disappointed sigh. "No one … sent me."

"I thought we were making progres, Ash," the man said. "I really did."

"Stop—"

The towel came down, followed a few seconds later by more water.

Ash felt the part of himself that had tasted the water split further away to observe as the water fell on his face and he choked and sputtered. It was like watching himself from the inside. Invisibly shaking his head in mock disappointment just like Left Arm Johnny. This time water did get up his nose. The claustrophobia was greater as the towel grew heavier from soaking up so much water, but also more contained, almost controlled.

Was this what it was like to drown? No. He knew it wasn't. Ash had almost drowned once, when he was twelve. In the deep end of a pool full of kids who didn't know he couldn't swim and hardly noticed him with all of the other kids splashing and diving and swimming around him. He had been thrashing. Swinging his arms and legs around. Trying to tread water with hands that weren't properly cupped, trying to grab the surface of the water and pull himself out. Trying to kick and move his body to the side of the closest side of the pool, where there might be a ladder or a leg or anything that he could grab. He had no idea how long it had been before his left hand scraped against the bottom rung of a ladder and he had been able to pull himself out of the water. All he remembered was the fight for his life had seemed to go on forever in agonizing slow motion.

He couldn't fight this. His arms and legs were secure. His hands clenched uselessly.

This wasn't drowning. This was what the murder victim felt after it had been rolled in a carpet and dumped off a bridge. Helpless in the water. Unable to fight. Uneable even to breathe. Unable to do anything as the alligators swam closer to investigate.

The water had stopped coming, but Ash didn't notice until the towel was lifted off his face.

"Hello there," Left Arm Johnny said, smiling. Then his smile went away. "Where were you, Ash? Who helped you? Who sent you?"

The questions came faster than Ash could hope to answer. He had time to take only a single breath. Then the towel was back in place and the water came again.

Ash's need to breathe seemed to ease as the water washed over him. As if the water was opening a gulf between his body and the part of him that observed what was happening to him. Water no longer poured into his nose. When Left Arm Johnny lifted himself up and dropped his weight on Ash's chest, the impact caused Ash to grunt in pain and expel the air in his lungs, but there was no coughing. No sputtering. Water was forced into his mouth, but he didn't breathe it, or even swallow it. It was just in his mouth.

When the water stopped flowing and the towel finally lifted, Ash turned his head and pushed the water out of his mouth with his tongue. Then he took a long breath.

"I'm not sure whether I should be pissed off, Ash, or impressed." Left Arm Johnny dropped the latest empty jug, then reached forward. He covered Ash's mouth with his left hand and gripped Ash's nose with his right, squeezing the nostrils shut. "How long can you hold your breath, Ash?"

Ash met the man's eyes. The calm part of his mind pushed the panicking part of him aside and settled in to find out.

Ash kept his eyes locked on those of Left Arm Johnny, but his attention was drawn to the faint pulse visible from the jugular vein on the man's neck. Left Arm Johnny's smile faltered after what had to have been a minute and was gone completely within another minute that Ash just stared at him, not breathing. Ash had no idea how he was holding his breath so long. The air in his lungs had to be going stale, but his lungs weren't burning. He wasn't getting lightheaded. He was just getting bored. He listened to Left Arm Johnny's heartbeat, feeling it through the man's fingers.

After what might have been five minutes, Left Arm Johnny released Ash's nose and pulled both hands back. Ash continued to stare at him. He didn't open his mouth or draw in a breath with his nose. In the living room, the TV was turned down and Big Man answered a phone call.

"Kid I knew in grade school could do that nose trick," Left Arm Johnny said. "Make his nostrils squeeze shut like that. But even he couldn't hold his breath for five minutes."

Ash realized his nostrils were squeezed shut. He opened them. A whiff of fresh air touched his nostrils, but he refused to breathe until he needed to. And he didn't seem to need to. Not yet.

After another minute of Ash and Left Arm Johnny watching each other, Sneer appeared in the door of the room. "You two lovebirds ready?"

"Fuck you," Left Arm Johnny said. "You should have seen—"

"Seen what? You guys making some kind of sex torture porno?" He turned left and right in an exagerrated show of looking around. "You got a camera hidden in here somewhere?

Wouldn't suprise me."

"Fuck you—"

"Shut up," Big Man said, pushing Sneer into the room, then following him in. "Mr. Derouen is on his way. Has Mr. Turner been appropriately softened up?"

Left Arm Johnny swung his leg over and stepped down from the bench.

Ash decided he should take the opportunity to breathe, whether he needed it or not. He took in a long, deep breath.

"You see that?" Left Arm Johnny said, pointing at Ash. "That son of a bitch can hold his breath for fucking ever. I've never seen anything like it."

"Is that a 'yes, boss'?" Big Man asked. "Or a 'no, boss, I fucked up, boss'?"

"It's not my fault you brought me a fucking fish."

"Does that mean I need to get the battery out of the van?" Sneer asked, sounding interested.

"No time for that, unfortunately," Big Man said. "Mr. Derouen is almost here. Just fill the jugs again and we'll all see how long he can hold his breath."

They didn't bother with the towel this time. Big Man, Sneer and Left Arm Johnny stood around Ash's head and dumped jug after jug of water on his face while Driver ran back and forth to the kitchen, refilling. Left Arm Johnny would tweak Ash's nose when the nostrils tried to close. Sneer punched him in the face or thumped him on the chest when Ash didn't sputter and choke enough to suit him.

Through the coughing and choking and the water in his eyes, Ash was still aware of the eyes watching from outside the window. He could almost feel the swamp pulling itself closer, as if to join in.

13

"WELL LOOK WHAT the gators spit back," Mr. Derouen said.

For the first time in his life, for the first time in two lives, Ash met Jamie's father. The man stood near enough that he had to bend his neck to look down at Ash. The color of Mr. Derouen's blue eyes was a match for Jamie's. The intense gaze had made the daughter look deep, intelligent, but made the father look cold, calculating. Like a snake.

Ash's right eye was swelling shut from Sneer's last punch, delivered right after Big Man had announced the arrival of Mr. Derouen. His nose hurt from being twisted almost off, his jaw had been bruised by multiple knuckles, and his tongue had found two loose teeth. He could taste his own blood. Human, coppery, warm. He had swallowed no water, though. Even when it had rushed through his nostrils, the chlorine stinging his sensitive mucus membranes, the water had just pooled in his mouth. Leaked out through his teeth as he grimaced against the pain of the beating.

He breathed normally as he met Mr. Derouen's gaze, as amazed as Sneer and Left Arm Johnny were pissed off that he could hold his breath as long as he could.

Big Man and Sneer stood behind Mr. Derouen. Big Man had his taser out, held in his right hand, but it wasn't activated. Sneer held his folding knife, the long blade extended and locked in place. He twirled the hilt of the knife through his fingers with practiced ease and smirking menace. Left Arm Johnny had been sent out of the room to turn off the TV. He hadn't returned. Ash had heard the man talking with someone else in a low voice, then silence.

"Why are you here, Mr.—" he paused and glanced back at Big Man.

"Mr. Turner, Mr. Derouen."

"Yes," Mr. Derouen said, drawing out the final "s" in a hiss. "Mr. Turner." His tongue touched his lips as if he was tasting the name. He focused on Ash again. "Why are you here, Mr. Turner?"

"I need to find Jamie," Ash said, the words coming out of him on their own.

Mr. Derouen's lips became a tight line. He glanced back at Big Man again.

Big Man looked embarassed for an instant, then he regained his composure. He gave a slight shrug. "That's all we were able to get out of him—"

"He said he has 'amnesia'," Sneer added. "If you can fucking believe that. I mean …" He let his words trail off as Mr. Derouen looked at him. It was the first time Ash had seen Sneer lose his signature expression.

Mr. Derouen looked down at Ash. "Do you even know who I am, Mr. Turner?"

"You are Jamie's father. Her rich father."

The man waved his hand in a gesture of dismissal, as if Jamie was the least important part of his life.

"And you're a controlling bastard," Ash added. "A rich, controlling bastard of a father. And probably an asshole."

Big Man stiffened, but didn't make any move. Mr. Derouen smiled, his lips pulling back to expose the tips of his teeth. Ash saw Jamie in that smile, and his fingers clenched.

"Yes," Mr. Derouen said, again drawing out the "s", "I can see you have been talking to Jamie, as well as fucking her. Oh, yes," he went on, his eyes moving to watch Ash's hands clench and unclench, "I'm well aware of the men in my daughter's life, and what they get up to with her." He paused, then looked Ash in the eyes again. "In fact, I count on it."

Ash looked back at the man.

"Disposable tourists like yourself, Mr. Turner, have been ..." He paused and glanced at the window, then back at Ash. " 'Interest payments' is probably the best way to put it." He let out a breath, almost a sigh. Ash smelled raw oysters and beer. "Sixteen years of interest payments. And now you."

Mr. Derouen leaned over so his face was close to Ash's. "Did you make a deal with the Devil, Mr. Turner? Is that why you're here? Is that how you came back?" When Ash didn't reply, he went on. "Despite how much I shouted at them, Mr. Turner, how big of a new asshole I might have ripped them when they told me you had come back, I don't have any doubt in their competence. If they said they shot you in the back of the head and left you floating dead in the bayou, I believe them. They did it, and you were. And yet ... Here you are. As if they didn't, and you weren't." He stood up straight again.

"In my experience, Mr. Turner, that kind of ... reversal of misfortune, let us say, requires a supernatural component." He started pacing, as if he were talking to a board of directors. "But not just *any* supernatural component, Mr. Turner." He gestured widely with his hands, encompassing the room, the house, and everything. "This is New Orleans, Mr. Turner. We have supernatural components of all shapes, sizes and colors. People who die here don't always stay dead, for whatever—

and *whom*ever—reasons. And so I'll ask again, Mr. Turner. Did you make a deal with the Devil?"

Ash just stared at him. Behind Mr. Derouen, Sneer crossed himself, the blade of his knife flickering from the rapid motion.

"It doesn't have to been the *actual* Devil, of course, Mr. Turner. In my own case—and, I suspect, yours, as well—it wasn't *the* Devil. Not even *a* devil. It was a god, Mr. Turner." Mr. Derouen smiled at Ash's reaction. "You don't believe me, Mr. Turner? Of all people, alive or dead or whatever it is you are now, I would expect *you* to believe me. Not *the* God, of course. But *a* god, yes." Mr. Derouen leaned close to Ash. "Do you remember your encounter with the god, Mr. Turner? I do."

Broken memories of teeth and claws flashed in Ash's mind, but he said nothing.

Mr. Derouen straightened and his expression became thoughtful. "I was an ambitious wildcatter in those days, Mr. Turner, but going broke. In desperation, I bought the used-up mineral rights for large sections of the swamp that were thought tapped out decades ago. I had an idea, Mr. Turner, a dream, if you will, that I knew how I could make those old, dried-up, dead sections of swamp pay out again. And pay out huge. Turns out, Mr. Turner, that I was right. But I was wrong first. You could even call me 'dead wrong', Mr. Turner." The smile of the snake touched the man's lips for an instant. Then he leaned in close to Ash again. "He was old, Mr. Turner," he went on, his breath warm on Ash's face. "And huge. An alligator straight out of a nightmare. He rose up on his hind legs and towered over me, his underside caked in rotting peat, his eyes as big as my hand and burning red. Is that how he looked to you, Mr. Turner? It doesn't shame me to say I shit my pants at the sight of him. I thought I was dead. Maybe I *was* dead, Mr. Turner. How can a living man talk to a god and survive? Of course," he added after a few seconds of silence, "you would have already been dead when you met him, wouldn't you, Mr. Turner?"

Mr. Derouen turned to Big Man. "Is there anything to drink here?"

Big Man looked at Sneer, who nodded and left the room. He came back with a bottle of whiskey and a single cup. He handed the cup to Mr. Derouen.

Mr. Derouen held the cup as Sneer splashed the brown liquid into the bottom. Ash's nose tingled at the strong alcohol scent with its hints of scorched wood.

Mr. Deouren took a sip, then said, "I was always a good negotiator, Mr. Turner, so that's what I did. I negotiated. And I started by asking for the Moon. I asked this god—the Egyptians called him Sobek, I learned later, though nothing about this god I saw resembled a man with the head of a crocodile—I asked him for the secret of how to pull more oil out of the dead swamps. Perhaps the god liked my audacity, my boldness, for he agreed to show me the secret places that still had oil. Then he told me what I would do for him. He wanted me to help restore his home to its former glory. I agreed. He wanted me to build a shrine to him in my yard. A small place of safety where he could observe the world that had grown up around him. I agreed. And he asked me for my firstborn child, in her thirteenth year. Yes, the god said 'her'. But I had no children then, Mr. Turner. I didn't even have a wife. My first wife had run away with my best foreman when he was offered a job at BP. So I agreed. Of course, I agreed.

"And the god ate me." Mr. Derouen smirked, the smug expression of a snake who has just swallowed a mouse. "I screamed, Mr. Turner, and I don't mind telling you. I thought I was dead. But then I woke up on a whithered island with the skeletal remains of dead cypress trees. I thought I had been dreaming, but then I *knew*. Mr. Turner, I *knew*. I had the secret. And where I had awoken amidst all that death from prior drilling in the swamps, I knew that I was standing on top of the largest pool seen in decades. The rest," he waved his hands to take in the house, the city, everything, "is history."

"You did not keep your part of the bargain," Ash said, the words almost pushing their way out of his mouth.

Mr. Derouen looked startled for an instant, and behind him Big Man and Sneer tensed. Then Mr. Derouen's smirk returned and the two men behind him relaxed.

"Yes, Mr. Turner. And no."

"So, no."

"Do not contradict me, Mr. Turner. I went so far as to create a small, man-made swamp on a secluded part of my property, with a cypress tree and a small statue of an alligator. Some nights I swear that statue came to life and roamed all over my property. More than once I saw it lurking in the shadows, watching my guests at garden parties. Further, Mr. Turner, I ploughed millions—*millions*, Mr. Turner—into efforts to restore the bayou. Flowers bloomed where nothing had grown in fifty years or more. It was beautiful, Mr. Turner. It was like the Garden of Eden reborn." He stopped, rage visible in his eyes and in the muscles clenched in his jaw, in his fingers on the glass. "Then it was all wiped out by one huge oil spill in the Gulf of Mexico. You probably heard about it. What was I supposed to do?"

"And your firstborn?"

Mr. Derouen's blue eyes locked on Ash's. "And what would you have done, Mr. Turner? No. I don't think so. There was no way I was going to give up Jamie. No chance. The day she was born, I destroyed the shrine. Ground the statue to powder, just to be safe. I drained the swamp and salted the ground. It's a blight now. A dead spot, like the island where

I had awakened. And I have never set foot in a swamp or bayou since that day. I didn't even let Jamie get on a boat, Mr. Turner." He stopped, glanced at the window, then looked at Ash again.

"When Jamie turned thirteen ..." He paused. "Nothing happened." He held his left hand palm up, almost a shrug. "There was no divine visit by an angry alligator god. No thunderbolts. No lightning. Nothing. I wondered if the god had died with its bayou in the same oil spill. Then her fifteenth birthday came. That's when the trouble started. At the pump sites. There were reports of alligators swarming. I saw video. It was ... Incredible, Mr. Turner. I assure you, you have never seen anything like it. Men died, or worse. I later learned that Jamie lost her virginity on the same night the first alligators were spotted crawling through storm-damaged fences. Can you believe that, Mr. Turner? My gator god was more interested in Jamie's sex life than I was." He took another sip of the whiskey. "But then I took an interest.

"The first one dumped Jamie less than three days after popping her cherry. Jamie was distraught. I'm sure you can imagine, Mr. Turner. I have no doubt you pulled off some similar stunt when you were a teenager. We all did. But this time, it was *my* daughter. I had this asshole found and delivered him at night to a pool near the dead island. I had him thrown into the pool. And there was peace again, Mr. Turner. Just like that. Peace and prosperity. For me and Jamie and Derouen Industries. For one year. And all it took was a little sacrifice. Hell, Mr. Turner, I wish Wall Street could be bought off so easily. But now ... here you are, Mr. Turner."

Mr. Derouen finished the glass, then held it out until Sneer took it. Mr. Derouen moved around Ash and placed his hands on either side of Ash's head. He leaned over until his face was directly over Ash's.

"I thought we had come to an agreement, Mr. Turner. For sixteen years, I've taken advantage of my daughter's capricious nature and throwaway Mardi Gras boyfriends. Growing up a party girl, it seems, had its advantages."

"No," Ash said. The memory of Jamie Derouen in his mind could not have been involved in anything like this.

"Oh, yes, Mr. Turner. She caught on by the time she was eighteen and pretty little Gary Martin disappeared. She had actually become somewhat attached to that one, it seems. My mistake. She understood, though, eventually. And she learned never to date anyone she wanted to keep around Mardi Gras." Mr. Derouen leaned over Ash. "You should have listened, Mr. Turner. She liked you as soon as she saw you. You should have called her *after* Mardi Gras, like she said. Or at least after poor, disposable Frank had tragically disappeared. But you were persistant, and she thought she could still have Frank pay the price." He sighed. "But I tried it with an old boyfriend once. Didn't take. It seems the taste of my daughter has to be ... Fresh. Or the old gator just isn't interested."

"Why are you telling me this?" Ash asked.

"Because except for Jamie, I've never told anyone, Mr. Turner. Not even my trusted associates here."

"You sound like a mad man."

"As someone who was dead a year ago, but who is now walking around, alive, obsessively focused on my daughter, I would expect more faith." Mr. Derouen paused. "So, Mr. Turner, I've told you my story. You tell me yours. Where have you been the last year?"

Ash looked up at him. "I don't know."

Mr. Derouen looked disappointed. He pushed himself back and away from the bench. "So you are only a pawn, Mr. Turner—"

"No," Ash said.

Mr. Derouen paused and looked down at him. Ash managed a smile that he hoped showed the blood in his mouth. He took a breath, then spoke the truth he had realized. The police detective had even told him. "I'm bait."

Red light like an angry sunrise shone through the window as a roar of wind that stank of decay and clotted blood shook the house like a tornado. The room's window burst in, bars bending, glass shattering, moldy drywall falling, as the ceiling was lifted away.

14

BIG MAN DROPPED his taser, reached into jacket, and brought out his gun faster than Ash had ever seen. Sneer still held his knife, but he had grabbed Mr. Derouen by the arm and was pulling him back as Big Man squeezed the trigger and fired over their heads. Three gunshots joined the cacophany of roaring and shouting. Ash could not see where the bullets hit the huge alligator that towered over them, but the beast roared even louder than before.

The creature's head, visible through the gaping hole where the ceiling had been, was as long as the bench Ash was still strapped to, and easily three times as wide. The one eye Ash could see glowed as red as an incinerator at full burn. The teeth were opposing rows of blackened hooks with points so sharp they were a blur. The alligator stood on its hind legs, its front claws still lifting the roof and ceiling while the rear legs tore at the wall.

The giant head thrust forward and the huge jaws closed on the wreckage of the roof. The neck and upper torso twisted and the roof was torn from the house and thrown away.

"Get him out of here!" Big Man shouted, then fired again, three shots. Then three more.

Ash watched the nearest rear leg rise in an arc, then come down hard enough to crash through the rotting wood of the floorboards. The impact pushed Ash and the bench he was tied to away from the huge claws.

Three more shots as the alligator took another step into the wreckage. Three more. The slide on Big Man's gun locked back. With a smooth, practiced motion, Big Man ejected the empty magazine and slammed another one in place. Behind him, Sneer was pulling Mr. Derouen through the door and the short hall.

The alligator god's other rear foot rose and came down just past Ash's feet, destroying more of the floor. The floor canted toward the god this time, causing Ash and the bench to slide nearer the creature. For the first time in hours, though, Ash's body was level with the ground. His vision blurred as the blood rushed out of his head.

The alligator god ignored Big Man's shooting, and ignored both Big Man and Ash as it tore away the next section of roof with its jaws. The left rear leg rose up and over Ash, then came down just past the bench, the long claws raking and slicing through Big Man from head to feet as the man inserted another fresh magazine. Blood splattered and the reloaded gun fell with the three main pieces of corpse.

The alligator god leaned and bent forward, reaching past the walls of the bedroom, out of sight.

The alligator god stood straight, holding Sneer in one hand and Mr. Derouen with the other. Sneer stabbed at the claws, but the knife slid off the scaled skin. The claw squeezed, bursting the man's torso, then dropped the remains.

Mr. Derouen struggled against the grip, looking up at the giant head. The alligator lifted Mr. Derouen so the man was at the end of the long snout, where both eyes could focus on him.

"Wait!" Mr. Derouen shouted. His left arm was pinned. He held up his right hand, palm outward. Still trying to negotiate. "Wait, please. We can work this out."

Hot breath steamed out of the nostrils on either side of the man as the red eyes of the alligator god looked at him.

"I will ... I will reinstate the bayou reclamation project," Mr. Derouen said. "I'll build you a fucking church—I mean, a cathedral. Or a shrine. Anything you want. Whatever you want. I'll build it right in the middle of the fucking French Quarter." Tears shone on his cheeks, reflecting the red of light that regarded him. "Please, I beg you. You ... You showed mercy before ..."

When the god did not respond, Mr. Derouen wiped at his cheeks with his free hand. "What do you want? Do you want Jamie? Do you want my daughter? Is that it? Have you come for her, finally?"

A growl in the chest of the god shook the ground, the air.

"Please, let me call her. She will come to me. She will help me. She will do this for me. Just let me ... Let me call her."

The jaws separated, the lower jaw dropping slowly.

"No! Please! Mercy, please. I will do whatever you want. Take Jamie! She's yours!"

The jaws stopped opening.

"See? I still have something you want. You want Jamie. I can get her for you—"

The great head thrust forward, the jaws snapping closed on Mr. Derouen's head and chest before he could even scream. With a jerk, the head pulled back, ripping the man in half. Ash felt a warm rain on his face as the rest of Mr. Derouen's body was thrust into the jaws with the head. There was no chewing. Only a toss of the head and a gulping swallow.

The giant tail of the alligator god swept over Ash as the creature turned around. The tail broke the remaining walls. Had the roof not already been gone, it would have fallen on Ash and crushed him. The alligator god took a step out of the wreckage, and walked through the overgrown backyard to the growing swamp.

"Wait!" Ash shouted.

The alligator god stopped. It twisted its head so that one red eye could look at Ash.

"What about me? What do you want from me?"

He expected words, and wondered what the voice of a god would sound like.

There were no words. Only a roar of fury and pain and betrayal that threatened both his eardrums and his mind. And with the roar, he remembered that he still needed to find Jamie Derouen. His whole being ached with that need. Every muscle in his body clenched and seized. If he hadn't been strapped to the bench, he might have folded himself in half and broken his own back.

Lightning flashed soundlessly in the charcoal gray sky, then the flickering white became pulsing red and blue and the crash of thunder arrived with a howl of sirens. The rain, though, didn't start until the first of the emergency response came through the gap in the wall where the window had once been.

15

ASH FELT COLD despite the blanket wrapped around his shoulders. He wondered, though, that he didn't shudder. The cold just made him sleepy. He pulled the blanket tighter around him, but the woven fibers had no warmth of their own to offer. They only contained and reflected what little warmth he could still feel inside. He sat on a plastic lawn chair that had been found in the backyard of the house, out of the rain under a canvas awning that had been raised beside the nearest ambulance. He could see police and firemen pulling at the wreckage of the house, looking for other survivors. Ash had tried to tell them there were no other survivors, but all he had been able to say was, "I need ... to find Jamie ... Jamie!"

When he had been inspected and determined to have no serious injuries, that the blood on him was not his own, he had been sat down, told not to move, and the policeman and EMT had rejoined the search.

He felt the warmth before he smelled the coffee or the wet man carrying it. The detective who had questioned him before appeared with two cups of coffee. The man's thinning hair and overcoat dripped with rain, but the disposable coffee cups were covered. Ash didn't wait to be offered. He held his hands out.

The detective hesitated for a fraction of a second, his eyes noting the lack of restraints on Ash's wrists, then gave Ash the cup in his left hand.

Ash held the cup with both hands, pulling it close to his chest, hunching over the warmth, holding the cup so the warm steam touched his face. He inhaled deeply.

"I knew when I watched you walk out the door this morning," the detective said, "that I would find you in someplace like this. Sooner or later. Usually, though, people like that try to make it so I find you 'later' more than 'sooner'. And, usually, they're not the ones who end up in the body bags."

"I need," Ash started. He forced himself to say, "I did not kill them."

"Of course you didn't. The EMT's say you were tied to a bench and there were signs of torture. They say there's no way you could've tied yourself to that bench."

Ash didn't answer. He focused on the coffee and its warmth.

"They also say you've got some bruises and maybe a busted rib or two," the detective said. He paused, as if considering whether he wanted to be good cop or bad cop, then settled for, "So you want to give your statement now?"

"I need," Ash started, but he closed his mouth, cutting off the rest of the alligator's god mission. Just the warmth of the coffee helped his mind unclench, allowed him to think past the compulsion. He could tell the detective what happened, though he didn't know if that would allow either of them to understand. Or even believe it. How was this going to be different from his last statement to the detective? Except he was no longer claiming amnesia.

He no longer doubted he had been dead, and brought back. With a purpose. Two purposes, actually. He had already fulfilled the first. What would he do about the second? How long could he fight it? Because there was no way he was going to betray Jamie, as her father had done.

He took in another deep, warm, aromatic breath, then took a cautious sip. "Yes," he said after swallowing. The warmth spread though his chilled insides and made it easier to think. To talk. "Now is fine."

The detective looked for a place to set his cup of coffee, found none and handed it to Ash. He extracted his notebook and a pen from inside his overcoat. "OK. Let's hear it then."

"First," Ash said, holding both cups close to his chest, "you have to know that ... Jamie—" Just saying her name, without getting up and leaving to find her was difficult, but Ash managed it. The coffee helped. "Jamie had nothing to do with this."

The detective kept his expression blank. "Go on."

Ash wondered how he would be able to live like this. Needing Jamie, feeling the urge to find her, to see her, to—He stopped the thought before his hands clenched and destroyed both cups of coffee.

"They grabbed me off the street," he said. "And they brought me here."

The effort made his hands shake, but he didn't drop the cups. Or crush them in his fingers. He could do this. He could fight it.

"They tortured me," he said. "They asked me ..." He paused, then went on. "They asked me the same questions you did. I told them the same thing I told you." *I need to find Jamie.* He managed not to say it.

He *would* fight. After all, what could the alligator god do to him now? Kill him again? Use him as bait again?

Ash smiled at the thought, and he glanced in the direction the alligator god had gone. He could not see the bit of urban swamp past the rain and the bright lights surrounding the wreckage of the house. Whether the alligator god saw him or noticed, Ash couldn't tell. But his smile made the detective stare at him even harder. He took another sip of his coffee, then told the rest of his story.

THE END
of
"Alligator Bait"
(Gator-man #1)

About the Author

David R. Michael was born a Yankee but raised all over the South, so he vehemently denies that he speaks with any accent whatsoever. He has been told, however, that many of his characters have a "soft Southern" accent, which really confuses him. They certainly didn't get it from *him*.

To know when new books by David R. Michael are available, and get a taste of what's coming up next, sign up for David's email newsletter here: **www.gunsandmagic.com**

ALSO BY DAVID R. MICHAEL

www.ingramcontent.com/pod-product-compliance
Lightning Source LLC
Chambersburg PA
CBHW020753130626
46554CB00006B/2165